# Walker's Journey Home

# WALKER'S JOURNEY HOME

## HELEN HUGHES VICK

*Harbinger House*

TUCSON

*In loving memory of*
*Helen Stokes Hughes and*
*Ruth Farmer Mecham*

Harbinger House
P.O. Box 42948
Tucson, AZ 85733-2948

Manufactured in the United States of America
∞ This book is printed on acid-free, archival quality paper.
Designed and produced by Whitewing Press, Tucson, Arizona.
Cover illustration by David Fischer

2  4  6  8  10  9  7  5  3  1

**Library of Congress Cataloging-in-Publication Data**
Vick, H. H. (Helen Hughes), date
Walker's journey home / Helen Hughes Vick.
p.  cm.
Sequel to: Walker of time
Summary: Still trapped in ancient times, fifteen-year-old Walker
reluctantly accepts the responsibility of leading a group of Indians
on a difficult and dangerous journey across the high desert country
of northern Arizona to a new home on the Hopi mesas.
ISBN 1-57140-000-1 : $14.95 -- ISBN 1-57140-001-X (pbk.) : $9.95
1. Sinagua culture--Juvenile fiction. [Sinagua culture-
-Fiction. 2. Hopi Indians--Fiction. 3. Indians of North America-
-Arizona--Fiction. 4. Time travel--Fiction.] I. Title.
PZ7.V63Wao  1995  [Fic]--dc20  94-39796

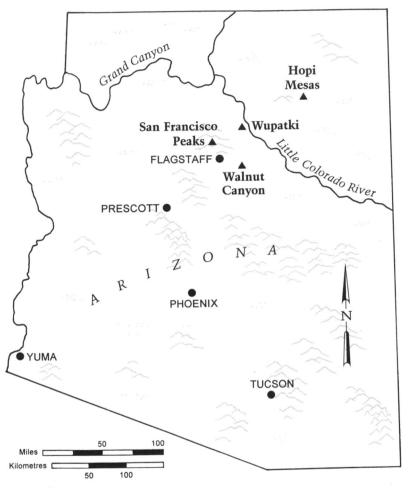

Grand Canyon

Hopi
Mesas ▲

San Francisco
Peaks ▲   ▲ Wupatki

FLAGSTAFF ●   ▲
Walnut
Canyon

Little Colorado River

PRESCOTT ●

A R I Z O N A

PHOENIX ●

N

● YUMA

TUCSON ●

Miles  [50   100]
Kilometres [
        50    100]

*The Land of*
*Walker's People*
SHOWING PRESENT-DAY CITIES

## Before . . .

"Find the cave . . . Open the back pack . . . Walk time . . . Time is very short . . . Do what must be done. Come home to Hopi."

Uncle Náat's dying request in 1993 changed forever the life of Walker Talayesva, a fifteen-year-old Hopi boy.

Walker and his Uncle Náat lived in a one-room adobe home without electricity or running water at the small, remote Hopi village of Mishongnovi on Second Mesa in northern Arizona. Náat raised Walker in all the traditional Hopi ways of seeking peace within yourself and those around you. Yet Náat also made Walker attend the white man's school to learn the bahana's ways, which were incongruent with the traditional Hopi life.

"You must learn the bahana's ways in order to help your people survive in the old ways," Náat said many times.

All his life, Walker felt like he was balancing on a tight-rope between the two opposing cultures and ways of life.

At Náat's dying request, Walker traveled to Walnut Canyon near Flagstaff, Arizona, where hundreds of mud-and-rock ruins of a mysterious, ancient people nestled under huge limestone ledges. Walker had no idea why Náat had sent him there nor what he was to do among the ruins of the ancient ones that the white man called the *Sinagua*.

During a fierce thunderstorm, Walker found the sacred cave and, inside, a barren rock shrine left by the ancient ones. In his backpack, he discovered a very old paho, or prayer stick. He sensed that the paho was the key to his purpose here. As Walker returned the paho to its rightful place on the shrine, the cave exploded with brilliant lightning, and a freckle-faced, curly haired white boy burst into the cave. The cave was instantly rocked with mind-shattering thunder and an all-consuming darkness.

Upon regaining consciousness, Walker discovered that he had walked back in time to the dangerous last days of the ancient ones. But he was not alone. Tag, the precocious son of a field archaeologist, had innocently walked along, too.

Together, Walker and Tag experienced living archaeology as they dwelled with the ancient people of the canyon who were struggling for survival against drought, hunger, and disease. Using their twentieth-century knowledge and skills, they helped the people through a plague only to become part of a deadly political struggle. Walker learned that he was the son of the dying high chief and had been brought back in time to become the ancient ones' new leader. Both Tag and Walker had to choose their own destiny—to stay in the thirteenth century or travel back into the twentieth century.

With regrets, Tag knew he must leave the ancient people he had come to love and try to get back to his own people. With no guaranty that he could return to his own place in time, Tag placed the paho on the holy shrine and walked back into the future, leaving Walker behind.

"Do what must be done. Come home to Hopi." Náat's dying words propelled Walker. He led the small band of desperate people out of the plague-stricken canyon to go to live with their brothers and sisters, the Hopi, on their mesas far to the northeast.

# Now . . .

What does the future hold for Walker in this era wrought with hunger, thirst, disease, superstition, and fear? Will his twentieth-century knowledge enable him to guide his people or will it cloud his judgment?

The lives and destinies of the ancient people rest on the shoulders of Walker of Time as he leads them on the journey home.

# 1

**B**lowing sand pelted Walker's face with a thousand blistering stings and sandpapered his bare legs and chest. His shoulder-length black hair whipped into his burning eyes. He tucked his head down. The thick sheet of blowing sand made the rocky, uneven ground difficult to see.

Holding on to Small Cub's thin shoulder, Walker moved the four-year-old boy forward. "Don't let go!" His words fought against the wind's roar.

Where were the others? Walker lifted his head to see. Sand filled his eyes and nose. It was hopeless. Even if his people were just a few feet behind, he couldn't see them. Walker fought the desperate feeling swelling in his heart. He clutched the eagle-shaped shell pendant that hung from a leather thong around his neck.

*Great Taawa, our creator, guide my people to safety.*

He struggled to keep his eyes open against the searing sand. The huge boulders that guarded the foot of the sacred mountain, the San Francisco Peaks, suddenly loomed ahead through the blowing sand.

*Shelter!*

Walker pulled Small Cub down beside a huge volcanic boulder. "Are you all right?" Sand whipped into his mouth. Grit ground between his teeth.

Small Cub nodded and leaned against the boulder to avoid the wind, but stray sand still stung his bone-thin body, clad only in a loincloth. Tucking his head down, Small Cub curled into a tight ball.

"Stay here. I've got to find the others." Walker lowered the large basket containing cornmeal, jerky, dried berries, and his few earthly possessions from his shoulder. He set it down next to the boy to form an additional windbreak. Small Cub looked up at Walker with fear in his dark, almond-shaped eyes. "I'll be back. I promise." Walker's words were carried off in the wind. He prayed he could keep his word.

Walker propped his long, wooden bow and heavy ceramic water jug against the basket. *If something does happen to me, Small Cub will at least have food and water.* He fought off the next logical thought—how long could a small boy survive alone in this desolate area? Worry for the others burned within Walker. He knew he had to take the risk and backtrack in hopes of finding them and leading them here to shelter.

"Taawa, protect your young son, Small Cub, and guide my steps," Walker prayed, moving away from the safety of the boulders. Shielding his eyes, he tried to see any of the people who had followed him out of the canyon. Five days ago his father, Chief Lone Eagle, had made him the new high chief. Lone Eagle died only minutes later, leaving all the responsibility upon fifteen-year-old Walker to protect and guide his people in their fight for survival.

True, there were others who could advise and help him. There was Great Owl, the old seer, whose powerful magic had sent Walker through time to the twentieth century to be raised. Great Owl's mysterious power had also brought Walker back in time to become high chief. White Badger, the nineteen-year-old warrior chief and Great Owl's son, would also help advise and lead the people. Yet Walker knew that the final decisions and responsibilities rested with him as high chief.

The sand whipped Walker's already raw flesh. "Great Owl, White Badger!" The wind's fury drowned his call. *Where are they? How could twenty-five men, women, and children just disappear?*

Walker chuckled. *Easy!* The blowing sand was as thick as fog. He called again. His words lashed back into his face. He moved on through the blistering sand with its stinging bullets.

How many of his people would be lost? The terrain was treacherous. Walker thought of Great Owl's old, spindly legs. A fall would snap the brittle bones, and broken bones with their complications meant almost sure death.

How were Morning Flower and Son of Great Bear protecting their infant daughter from the deadly sand? What about all the other children? How many families would be separated in the blinding storm? Each of his people's faces streaked across Walker's mind. Worry rose in his throat like bile. He hoped that White Badger, who always covered the rear position, had kept anyone from getting separated at his end.

*I certainly didn't. What kind of leader am I, losing all my*

7

*people?* If he couldn't get his people through a sandstorm, how could he even hope to lead them to the Hopi mesas ninety miles away?

The ground gave away beneath Walker's yucca sandals. He landed spread-eagled on the knife-sharp volcanic rocks. Tears of frustration washed the sand from his eyes. Pain lashed his body as he struggled to his feet against the battering wind.

*It is hopeless! I was a fool not to go back into the future with Tag.* How could he lead these desperate people? His twentieth-century, white man's schooling hadn't included classes in surviving sandstorms, hunger, thirst, or insects that ate you alive or in any of the other thousand daily requirements for survival in A.D. 1200 and something. Even Uncle Náat's tireless training in the Hopi traditions and ways was useless at this minute.

"Walker of Time, take your people home," Náat's voice seemed to cry in the wind's sharp howl.

Walker grasped his pendant. "Then help me, Uncle!" The wind whipped his anger back into his face.

A shadow moved in front of him. Walker reached out and made contact with coarsely woven cotton. *Great Owl!* Realizations flashed through Walker's mind. If Great Owl could see into one's soul and into the future, then he could easily see through the blistering sand. Walker put his arms around the stooped man. "Where are the others?" his words battled the wind.

Great Owl lifted his carved wooden staff. Walker saw a red cord tied to it. Another shadowy figure materialized through the curtain of sand, followed by a second, and a third, each holding the red lifeline.

"There is shelter ahead." Embarrassment consumed Walker. Of course Great Owl knew this. It was *Great Owl* who had led the people to safety using his seeing powers, as well as common sense.

Great Owl took Walker's arm and pulled him close. Over the wind's roar he said, "My son, you must use your eyes, the inner sight deep within you, to guide you."

Walker's body jerked. His eyes filled with stinging sand as he stared at Great Owl. What was he saying? Inner sight?

"At first it will be as the blowing sand in the whirling wind," Great Owl gripped Walker's arm with surprising strength, "but you must work hard to *see* what lies ahead for you and your people."

Walker's mind rocked with shocked confusion. Had he heard Great Owl's word correctly? What inner sight did Great Owl mean? Certainly not the power to see into the future, but yet . . . The wind raged around Walker as his thoughts boiled within. It was all too much to comprehend. He couldn't think about it now.

Walker helped Great Owl and his fifteen-year-old daughter, Flute Maiden, settle down beside Small Cub. Flute Maiden pulled a turkey feather blanket over her and Small Cub. Great Owl huddled under his long, red cape.

One by one, the others settled in against the nearby boulders. Arrow Maker, his wife, and their four children were followed by Fawn, Rising Sun, and their baby son. Gray Dove, Quiet Wind, and their children came all in a bunch. Relief flooded Walker as Scar Cheek, Littlest Star, and their preteen sons and teenage daughter appeared through the sand. Walker heard Morning Flower's infant daughter's cry before he saw her appear through the curtain of sand. Her husband, Son of Great Bear, was at her side. "Small Cub?" his worry rose above the wind's blustering cry.

"With Flute Maiden." Walker pointed with his chin.

White Badger appeared last. Seeing his friend and second in command, Walker felt relief.

"We thought we had lost you and Small Cub!" White Badger shouted. His strong body stood against the searing sand and wind.

"We weren't lost. You were," Walker joked, but his words vanished in the wind. He led the way back to Great Owl. White Badger knelt beside his father, sheltering the old seer with his own body. Flute Maiden held up her blanket. Walker ducked under and plopped Small Cub in his lap.

Walker settled down, wrapping his arms around Small Cub. Love and gratitude filled his heart. His people were together and safe for the moment.

*Kwa kwa, thank you, great Taawa,* Walker prayed silently.

He could feel Flute Maiden's thin body huddled against his own. Walker looked into her oval-shaped face. Even coated in sand, it was beautiful. The deeply slanted, almond-shaped, black eyes reflected his own worry. "The others are all safe." Her soft voice held uncertainty, making the statement a polite question.

Walker nodded. Of course Flute Maiden shared his concern for everyone. She had helped bring all the younger children into the world and had treated their parents at one time or another with her herbal teas, medicines, ointments, and love. Flute Maiden smiled at Walker. Her smile said she was glad—glad everyone was safe, glad to be with him.

Small Cub squirmed in Walker's lap. "Where are Mother and Father?"

Walker held him close. "They are just a few steps to the east with your baby sister, Small Light. They are all as snug as bugs in a rug."

"You say funny things, just like Tag." Small Cub looked up. "I wish Tag were still here. I liked him, even though he was speckled like an egg and had hair like the whirling wind."

A freckled face with a toothy grin appeared in Walker's mind. *Trumount Abraham Grotewald—Tag.*

"So do I, Little Brother." Walker swallowed the lump in his throat and realized just how much he missed the friendly, curly haired bahana who had accidentally walked back into time with him. He had never had any white friends before Tag. Bahanas were just a bunch of loud, pushy, know-it-alls who pitted their strange, competitive ways against the peaceful, harmony-seeking ways of the Hopi. But in Tag, Walker found a loyal friend with inner strength and an understanding heart.

Worry gnawed at Walker. Would Tag ever make it back to his Mom and Dad, or would he walk time endlessly? *Great Taawa, please guide your white son back to . . .*

Small Cub's bony elbows dug into Walker's ribs. "I'm hungry."

"So am I, but we'll have to wait until this sandstorm blows over." Walker squeezed Small Cub. "You wouldn't want to have sand in your food." Small Cub laughed and snuggled in closer. Sand or finely ground rocks in food was an everyday occurrence here, since all corn, the main staple of life, was ground on large, troughed stones called metates.

Small Cub squirmed again. "Yaponcha, the God of the winds, must be angry at us for leaving our canyon and homes."

"No, I am sure that Yaponcha is glad that we left since Masau'u, the God of death, has claimed the canyon for his own.

Yaponcha is being kind by hiding us from Masau'u. Even powerful Masau'u wouldn't come hunting for us in this storm."

Small Cub reached up and touched Walker's eagle pendant. "Tell me again where we are going." His voice held uncertainty.

Walker felt Flute Maiden move against his shoulder. Though she had her head tucked down, he knew she was listening as intently as her nephew. He felt her apprehension.

Walker began, "Northeast of here, many days' journey, are long, flat-topped mountains."

"I have never seen mountains with flat tops. The sacred mountain has pointy tops," Small Cub interrupted. "How can mountains have smooth tops?"

Walker's voice took on a storyteller's quality as he spoke over the wind's blare. "When this, the fourth world was created, Spider Woman and Taawa knew that the good people would someday need to live high on mountains for their protection. So they created rocky-sided mountains with flat tops.

"Then our forefathers' clans climbed out from the holy sipapu, the hole in the earth, into this, the fourth world. Taawa lead them on a sacred migration that took them in the four directions across the great land. Finally Taawa guided them to the rocky canyon where our people built their homes and lived for many generations." Walker paused. "Our brothers, the Hopi, the People of Peace, also climbed up through the sipapu with our forefathers. But Taawa lead the Hopi to the flat-top mountains, where they built their homes and planted their corn."

"And that is where we are going, to the flat-top mountains of the Hopi," Small Cub repeated the words Walker had told him many times since they left their rock-and-mud cliff homes of Walnut Canyon.

"Yes, we will go there and ask our brothers if we can live beside them."

"Will the Hopi people let us stay with them?"

Walker's stomach twisted. Would the ancient Hopi let his small band of people settle upon their land? It was a question that he had asked himself so many times that now it was like a canker sore in his mind.

He felt sure this was one of the reasons that as a young child he had been sent into the future with his uncle, Náat, so that he could be raised in the traditional ways of the Hopi at a Hopi village. Walker knew that when they reached the mesas, his traditional Hopi lifestyle and beliefs would be invaluable. Even though his people's culture was surprisingly similar to the Hopi's, there would still be many adjustments to make in order to live side by side with the Hopi. Walker would be not only his people's leader, but also their teacher and example in assimilating the Hopi way of life.

Small Cub's voice penetrated Walker's anxious thoughts. "But will the Hopi let us stay?"

Walker felt Flute Maiden's worried eyes resting on him also. They both needed the reassurance that only he could give them. His stomach twisted again. Could he honestly give it? Would the Hopi today, somewhere between A.D. 1200 and 1300, maybe later, be willing to share their limited resources? That is, if and when he could get his people to the mesas.

He rested his chin on Small Cub's soft, but gritty black hair. "Oh-ay, yes, little brother, I believe so. That is why I came back, to lead you all home to Hopi."

The future of his people lay in his hands.

# 2

Walker looked out over the panoramic vista of prairie and sky interrupted by cinder hills, volcanic buttes, and pink mesas far to the northeast. The noonday sun beat down on the vast land, staining it in harsh hues of grays and browns. Though the scene was stark, Walker felt the beauty and balance of nature before him. Peace seeped into his heart. He had come full circle.

He had seen this same vista before—some seven hundred years in the future. Vivid memories filled his mind in a maze of colors, smells, thoughts, feelings, and perceptions. He had come with his eighth-grade class to Wupatki National Monument, as it was named then, to visit the ruins of the ancient people that the Hopi called *hisatsinom*.

On that spring day in 1993, Walker had felt something deep within himself stir as if waking from a dream. The wind teased Walker's nose with the fragrance of spring wildflowers as he climbed out of the school bus to take in the view. It was good to stretch and breathe fresh air after being in the bus all morning. Walker worked his way through the giggling, flirting girls and encouraging boys. He escaped to the edge of the view point for a few minutes of space and time alone.

The wide-open space enveloped him as the sounds of his classmates were lost in the spring breeze. The beauty was unbelievable. The endless miles of open grassland were broken up by prominent rock formations of black lava. In eerie contrast, streaks of brilliant red sandstone snaked under the shelves of the black basalt rock.

Standing alone, Walker stretched and took a deep breath. The smell of smoke entered his nose. Where was it coming from? Walker swung around in a circle, searching. There was no smoke curling through the air, yet his nose burned with it. The hair on his neck stood up, and a crawling sensation spread across the back of his shoulders.

"Come on, everyone. Get back on the bus," called Mr. Glitch, the large, authoritative bahana teacher in charge of the field trip. "The ruins of the ancient ones await us. It's time to walk back into the past."

. . . *time to walk back into the past.* The words echoed in Walker's mind. Unfamiliar faces flashed through his mind like lightning—perceived but not really seen.

"Walker," Mr. Glitch's loud voice called. "The others are waiting for you."

. . . *the others are waiting for you.* The words thundered through Walker, leaving him shaking in a cold sweat. What is happening to me? he wondered, forcing his wobbly legs back to the bus.

Walker knew now—wearing a leather loincloth, simple yucca sandals, and with his people sitting nearby—what had really happened that day hundreds of years in the future. Now he recognized the faces that had flashed through his mind that day. They were friends from the past. Mr. Glitch had been correct; the others had been waiting for him to come back into time to assume his rightful place as their leader.

Walker brought his thoughts and eyes back to the present. He shifted the leather strap of the water jug on his left shoulder. Yes, the others were waiting for him, but could he lead them to safety? The images of shallow, rocky graves began invading Walker's mind. He fought against the apparition. Turning to White Badger, he said, "It's about time to move on."

"Just a bit longer," White Badger suggested. His voice was calm, as always. "We've come a long way already today."

Walker lowered the basket from his right shoulder to the ground. White Badger was correct. It had taken all morning for the band to travel as far as a car or bus in the future could go in minutes. *If only we had a bus to . . .* Walker pushed the unrealistic wish from his mind. Best to concentrate on this minute in time, he told himself.

Squatting, Walker studied his people gathered in small, family groups nearby. The younger children chased each other. Even after five days of walking, it was all still a new and wonderful adventure for them. The older children sat listening to their parents talking with one another. Walker's heart warmed as he watched the adults visiting. They were good people—people seeking peace within themselves and harmony and balance with those around them.

Flute Maiden caught his eye. She was kneeling beside Arrow Maker, rubbing his uneven legs with ointment. A smile flashed across her face as she looked at Walker for an instant before lowering her eyes to her work. "This will help loosen the sore muscles and keep the insects away, too," her musical voice carried in the breeze.

Walker knew that Flute Maiden's touch was soothing to both the body and the soul. How could one so young and lovely be so wise in so many things? he wondered. Yet she was not so young, Walker realized, glancing at the other women with their families. Age was accelerated and life shortened by the constant struggle for daily existence. At fifteen, Flute Maiden was more than of marriageable age. Most women her age had at least one child. Why hadn't she married yet? She was far more beautiful than the others. Being the daughter of Great Owl and sister to the warrior chief gave her high social status, yet she was still a maiden. Walker was flooded with a mixture of emotions that made him feel hot and cold, jealous, yet distant, all at the same time. *What—or who has she been waiting for?*

Walker forced his uncomfortable thoughts and eyes to Arrow Maker with his long yellow cape and confident eyes. How had Arrow Maker, with his humped back and uneven legs, been able to keep up with the others? Walker felt very fortunate to have Arrow Maker with them. He not only had inner strength and courage, but was an expert stone knapper. Good knives, arrows, and spears were critical to life and Arrow Maker made the best. These and the other items Walker's people made were valuable commodities to trade, and this bartering power would be essential for their survival.

Arrow Maker's wife, Early Snow, sat close by. She had the same inner strength as her husband and an accepting nature that matched her pleasing face and beautiful dark eyes. Arrow

Maker and Early Snow had four energetic but mannerly children ranging from eight to thirteen years old. Early Snow's thin body was covered, like the rest of the women's, with a short woven skirt and a blouselike cover that wrapped over one shoulder, leaving the other shoulder bare. Walker had not yet figured out what kind of fiber had been used to make most of the women's clothes and many of the men's loincloths. He'd have to remember to ask Flute Maiden about that.

Walker's eyes moved on to the others eating pinion nuts and visiting. Fawn, sixteen, was taking her son from his wooden cradle board. Already the lower back of his little head was flattened from being strapped into the cradle board for hours at a time. He fussed until he found his mother's milk. Walker smiled. Fawn was a gentle mother and expert potter whose creations were not only practical, but had a graceful beauty that set them apart. Rising Sun, Fawn's young husband, was a skilled farmer and master carver in bone and wood. Walker enjoyed carving himself and appreciated watching Rising Sun work. He doubted he'd ever be the artisan Rising Sun was, but he was learning.

Quiet Wind, a small, sturdy man, sat close to Rising Sun. Both he and his wife, Gray Dove, an equally petite woman, created beautiful clothes, moccasins, bags, and other items from pelts, skins, and hides that they cured to velvety softness. They were a quiet, loving couple who had three vibrant and hard-working children.

Walker shifted his weight and let his eyes moved to Littlest Star, a pretty woman with a patient nature. Weaving baskets, mats, and other useful items from yucca was her specialty, along with raising her children. Her fingers were seldom still. Scar Cheek, with a long, angry scar cutting across his reddish-brown, square face, was talking to their eldest son in a quiet but firm voice. He was a skilled farmer and sandal maker. His carrying basket contained yucca cordage and other materials needed to repair or make new sandals for his people. Walker was glad that Scar Cheek had chosen to come, not just because he would keep the people in footwear, but because Scar Cheek was a strong, kind person whom Walker could trust and depend on.

Morning Flower smiled at Walker and lowered her eyes to the infant at her breast. She was Great Owl's oldest daughter—twenty, beautiful, and extremely shy. Her husband, Son of Great Bear, sitting nearby, was just the opposite with his self-assured confidence. His strong inner peace and harmony were evident to all. Of all the people, Son of Great Bear seemed to be most in balance with the world around him. He was the inventor of the group, creating ingenious tools from stone, bone, and wood that amazed even Walker's twentieth-century mind. Walker treasured Son of Great Bear's friendship and counsel.

Walker shifted his gaze to Great Owl, who sat on a large rock apart from the others. A clam-shaped shell studded with small, square pieces of turquoise hung from his thin neck. Like the other men, he was bare except for a loincloth. Looking at Great Owl's spindly legs, Walker wondered if they could carry him the entire way to the mesas. How old was Great Owl? Walker couldn't even guess. His face was deeply wrinkled, and his waist-length hair was white, but his deep brown eyes were timeless.

Great Owl had not spoken again of Walker's inner sight, and Walker had not brought up the subject, although he knew that he must sometime. Just being high chief, with all the attendant authority, countless decisions, and ever-present worry—along with the minute-by-minute struggle against thirst and hunger, was overwhelming. Walker couldn't face the possibility of becoming a seer. Besides, they had Great Owl, he told himself. *But if something happened to Great Owl, how could I ever* . . . Walker pushed the thought—the fear—out of his mind as a cold shiver crept up his back.

Walker forced his attention to focus on White Badger, who stood nearby. His face was square in shape and his features strong. Below straight bangs, his jet black eyes reflected quick intelligence. He was the same height as Walker, five foot four, and they usually saw things eye to eye. With his open, friendly ways, common sense, and good judgment, White Badger handled his authority with self-assured dignity. Without White Badger as warrior chief, many more of the people would have stayed behind.

At the thought of those remaining at Walnut Canyon, Walker's throat tightened. For one reason or another, nearly half the people at Walnut Canyon had refused to leave their comfortable stone-and-mud cliff homes. A clever but dangerous young man named Gray Wolf was now their leader. How long could they survive with tainted water, crops dying from thirst, and not enough food for the coming winter? Walker's own aunt, Singing Woman, had chosen to remain behind because of her old age and sightless eyes.

Walker closed his eyes. *Taawa, please be with those staying behind.* Tears welled up behind his closed eyelids. How long could Singing Woman live without someone bringing her food and water?

"We should be able to reach Strong House before sunset." White Badger's comforting voice brought Walker's eyes open. "You can see it from here." He pointed with his square chin.

Walker stood and stretched his cramped legs. He could make out the walls of the huge, fortlike pueblo sitting on top of a steep, black cinder hill a few miles below. Gray smoke circled into the brilliant sky from the pueblo. "You said you have been there before."

"Just once, when I was very young. We visited Strong House on our way to trade at Tall House." White Badger paused, remembering. "I'd never seen such a huge structure before, two houses high, with endless rooms."

"He managed to examine most of the rooms." Great Owl moved up next to his son. He leaned heavily on his carved staff, but his large eyes twinkled. "I thought we had taught him better manners, but an old grandmother from the Parrot Clan taught him about respecting the privacy of others."

White Badger chuckled and rubbed his backside. "A lesson I have never forgotten."

"I hope that *they* have short memories," Walker teased. "We are going to need all the hospitality we can get."

Great Owl gazed toward Strong House. His long, white hair was pulled back and tied at his neck. A few stray strands danced around his face in the breeze. "In years past, visitors were welcomed at all the different villages. This area was known as a place to trade everything—food, tools, birds, shells," Great Owl paused, "even ideas and new ways. People came from as far away as the great waters to barter." He shook his head and leaned on his staff, which was carved with intricate designs. "Now the area is becoming barren. The clouds have become hardened against it. They do not share their rain with the dying crops. Yaponcha enjoys blowing all the black, moisture-holding cinders off the farm fields, so the crops wilt in the hot sun. More people have left to seek a kinder place to plant their crops than have stayed to struggle for life."

Walker remembered the many small, five- to twelve-room pueblo villages they had seen in the last five days. The abandoned stone houses stood as lonely monuments of the long drought that had been forcing a great exodus from the area.

Great Owl turned to Walker. His eyes were intent. "Many of the clans at Strong House have left. Those remaining are friendly, but they struggle for food and water just as we did in our canyon."

*Will they let us stay with them long enough for us to prepare for the rest of our journey?* Walker wanted to ask, knowing that Great Owl could see into the future. Instead, he listened to the wind singing around them, afraid to even try seeing into the future himself.

Great Owl continued, "My grandfather's people came from a small village northwest of Strong House called Lomaki."

"Lomaki—Beautiful House," Walker said. "The people of your father's clan may be more hospitable than those at Strong House."

Great Owl did not respond, but the corners of his mouth turned up slightly. Walker had his answer. They would stay at Lomaki long enough to barter and gather essentials for their journey to Hopi. Yet something deep in Great Owl's eyes warned Walker that life at Lomaki was not going to be all beautiful.

What lay ahead for his people in this windswept valley of abandoned homes and lives? A deathly coldness crept into Walker's heart.

# 3

The sun was low in the western sky by the time Strong House stood high above Walker and his people. Strong House was an impressive sight sitting on top of a steep, black cinder butte. The pueblo village looked like a huge castle or fort with its massive red walls made of sandstone slabs skillfully trimmed and mortared together with mud. Here and there, interrupting the neat red slabs, were large, coarse, black lava rocks. A few small, rectangular windows in the second story and one narrow entrance were the only visible openings in the high, protective walls.

*Citadel,* the name that the archaeologists of the future would give this village, fits it well, thought Walker. The memory of what this magnificent structure looked like in seven hundred years streaked across his mind. A cold shiver raced up his back, pulling at the nape of his neck. Strong House would be nothing more than a few tumbled down walls—just rubble on a hill whipped by the wind that whispered of times of the past. Walker closed his eyes and tried to block out the haunting images.

"I'm tired of waiting." Small Cub tugged on Walker's arm. "Let's just go up into the village."

"It is not polite to go in uninvited. We must wait here until our message is delivered to the high chief. If the clan leaders will let us stay, they will send word," Walker said, squeezing the boy's shoulder. It would be dark soon, and they had hoped to stay here for the night before going on to Lomaki.

Small Cub looked up. "What if they won't let us stay?"

"We will have to . . ."

A middle aged man dressed in a white kilt appeared on the steep path that led up to the village. A long strand of turquoise beads hung on his bare chest. The man's step was fast and his smile bright.

"It's Leaning Tree, the high chief," Great Owl said, moving up next to Walker. Great Owl now wore his red, knee-length ceremonial kilt, decorated with small, white shells, and his skullcap, beaded with thousands of colorful beads that glittered in the fading light.

"Welcome, Great Owl." Leaning Tree's voice was warm. His long hair, tied at his neck, was streaked with gray, and his round face was lined with distinction.

"It is good to see you." Great Owl held out his left hand, resting on his staff with his right.

Leaning Tree bent down and blew on Great Owl's open hand in a sign of greeting and respect. "It has been too many seasons since we have talked face to face, my friend."

Great Owl nodded and turned toward Walker. "This is our new high chief, Walker, son of Lone Eagle."

Leaning Tree extended his large hand. "We would be honored if your people would join us for the night."

With respect and gratitude, Walker leaned over and blew on the man's open hand. For at least one night his people would sleep in safety.

Within the high, enclosed walls of Strong House, the open air plaza was busy. It was a good sized courtyard, with many low, T-shaped doors opening into it. Smooth pole ladders leaned up against the rough walls to the second-story hatchways. A few taller ladders reached up to the roof. The right pole on every ladder was shorter than the left side, making climbing off the ladder easier. Beside a few first-story doorways, women sat visiting, their hands still busy with daily tasks. Young children, naked except for a necklace or bracelet, played in noisy groups. Their laughter echoed within the closed walls. As Walker and his people entered, the children's laughter died. They stopped to stare at the strangers for a minute, then continued on with their games as if accustomed to visitors in their village.

Across the plaza, a group of women gathered in a flurry of movement carrying large ceramic bowls of food and flat baskets stacked with corn cakes. A short woman with smiling eyes left the throng and hurried toward Walker's people. She mirrored the other women in her short, one-piece, dark dress that draped over her right shoulder, exposing her left. A strand of small shells hung from her neck, and dainty shell loops hung from her ears. Hair combs, carved from deer leg bones, pinned her thick, dark hair in a knot at the back of her head. "Welcome," her happy voice carried over the children's noise. She reached down and scooped up a toddler who had stumbled in a heap in her path. Slinging the child onto her hip, she hurried up to Flute Maiden. "I am Leaning Tree's wife, Morning Talk. My husband has told me of you and your respected family. We would be honored to have the women and children eat with us while the men talk."

"Thank you for your kindness," Flute Maiden said. She smiled at the small, wide-eyed child on Morning Talk's hip and petted his chubby arm. "I hope we can repay you in some way."

"It is our honor." Morning Talk slipped her free arm through Flute Maiden's. "We are anxious to hear all the news from your canyon." They started across the plaza to where the bowls and baskets of food were being arranged on ground mats in front of the houses.

Flute Maiden looked over her shoulder and smiled at Walker, giving him her support in what he faced with the clan leaders. The other women began pairing off and visiting with village women as well. Walker watched, amazed at the friendliness of the women. Would the men be as accepting?

"Just leave your baskets and things here. The men are waiting in the kiva." Leaning Tree started toward the east side of the plaza to where the top of an uneven log-pole ladder protruded from the ground through a hatchlike opening. The ladder led down into the kiva, the religious and social gathering place of the men. It was considered to be the very heart of the village.

Great Owl's cold fingers touched Walker's arm as Leaning Tree disappeared down the kiva ladder. He whispered, "You must be careful. Let Taawa guide your thoughts and words, my son. All is not as it seems here."

The logs of the ladder felt smooth under Walker's sweaty hands as he climbed down into the dimly lit kiva. The air felt

26

cool and close. Standing away from the ladder in the center of the kiva, Walker looked around the large, keyhole-shaped room. Other than the shape, it was very similar to the Hopi kivas of the future, with its white plaster walls decorated with a wide variety of designs. Walker had spent countless hours in just such a kiva, practicing for Kachina dances, receiving religious instruction, visiting, and listening to the men's stories and legends. He, as most other males, had slept many nights in the serenity of his clan's kiva.

A low stone bench circled the kiva walls. About twenty men sat on the bench or on the mat-covered floor. Most wore loincloths, but a few older men wore long kilts decorated with beads or shells. *Clan leaders.* He felt all eyes on him. Even though it was rude to stare, there were ways to inspect a person without being offensive, and Walker knew he was being scrutinized by each man in the room. He kept his eyes from meeting anyone else's while the others descended the ladder.

Walker sat down beside Great Owl and White Badger on the hard, cool stone bench. Fading daylight shone through the ladder's hatch in the roof. Ceramic bowls filled with fat and floating wicks helped illuminate the kiva. The smell of sweaty bodies filled the room. The air buzzed with talk. As one last man descended the ladder, the chatter stopped abruptly. Tension streaked with animosity and fear permeated the air. Walker could tell that every man present felt it. No one looked at this young man who sat on the matted floor apart from the others, yet everyone in the room was very conscious of him.

Leaning Tree stood. "Friends and leaders of our village, we are honored to have visitors from the rocky canyon from the south sharing our hearth this night." His deep voice filled the kiva, easing the tension. He turned to Walker.

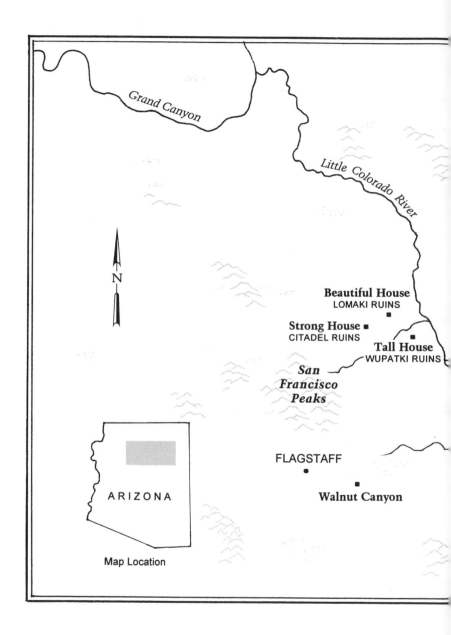

Grand Canyon

Little Colorado River

N

Beautiful House
LOMAKI RUINS

Strong House ■
CITADEL RUINS

Tall House
WUPATKI RUINS ■

San
Francisco
Peaks

FLAGSTAFF

Walnut Canyon

ARIZONA

Map Location

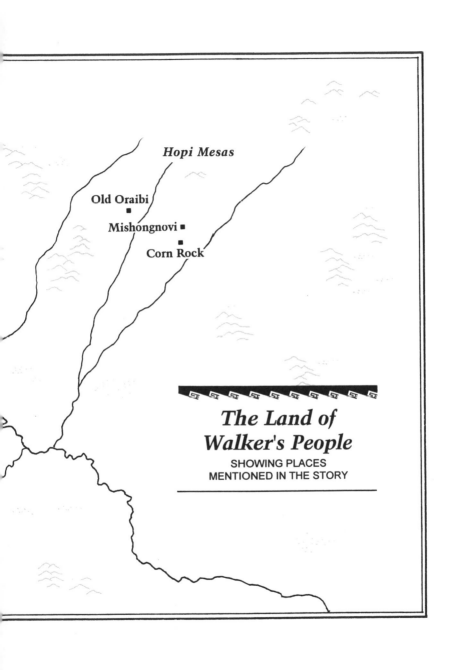

Hopi Mesas

Old Oraibi

Mishongnovi

Corn Rock

*The Land of Walker's People*

SHOWING PLACES
MENTIONED IN THE STORY

"As high chief of Strong House, I welcome you, Walker, son of Lone Eagle. We are saddened at the news of the passing of your father. He was a man of great leadership and inner strength. May you follow in his footsteps."

Swallowing the knot of grief in his throat, Walker rose. "Kwa kwa, thank you, for your kindness. My people are weary from our journey. We appreciate your hospitality. Each of us will find a way to repay your kindness in some way." Walker saw the heads of his men nod. The men of Strong House responded with confirming nods and sighs.

"Great Owl, our spiritual leader and seer, has offered his assistance to your people." The kiva again filled with sighs and nods. Great Owl's powers were well known and accepted among these men. Walker knew that many would seek out Great Owl for advice and counsel, and his people's debt would be less.

"That is a very generous offer, young man." The voice was courteous yet contemptuous.

Without looking, Walker knew it was the man who had brought tension and fear into the kiva. He glanced in the man's direction. Cold, hard eyes met his with a glare that dared him to look away.

"Where much is offered, much is wanted." The man was about twenty-two years old. His straight, blue-black hair hung free to his broad shoulders. He wore a plain white loincloth, but his muscular chest was covered with a massive turquoise necklace. Matching loops of fine turquoise hung from his ears, and both of his wrists supported turquoise bracelets. Walker had never seen such a strikingly handsome face before, with its clean lines, classic nose, and square chin and forehead. The man's skin was almost fair compared to darker men around him, making him stand out as an exotic foreigner. His dark eyes spoke of a quick, determined intelligence. "Perhaps the son of Lone Eagle has needs that are beyond what the people of Strong House can give."

The hair on Walker's neck stood up.

"Silent Thunder, since you do not live at Strong House, you should not be concerned with what my people can offer our visitors." Leaning Tree's voice was firm. Static jumped between the two men. "You, too, are a *guest* in our kiva."

"As always," Silent Thunder answered, "I am grateful to you for letting me come to Strong House to trade, even though it is not as profitable as at Tall House or even the smaller villages."

Leaning Tree was thrown off by the statement as if it were a threat. Whatever political game Silent Thunder and Leaning Tree were engaged in, Walker realized that he didn't want his people caught up in it.

Walker looked at Great Owl, who was studying Silent Thunder. No hint of what he was seeing or thinking showed on his face. He knew Great Owl was leaving the situation up to him.

Unlike his father, White Badger reflected visible concern and distrust. He met Walker's eyes, warning caution.

"Leaning Tree, my people's needs are simple for the night, a bit of food and water and a protected place to sleep." Walker saw uncertainty flicker in Leaning Tree's eyes, or was it something else? Walker hesitated, then went on, "Tomorrow we will go to Lomaki."

Thick silence consumed the kiva. Fear showed openly on all faces. Some exchanged nervous glances. Many eyes were cast downward in prayer. Walker tried to swallow the knot rising in his throat. What had his people walked into?

The uncomfortable silence was shattered by Silent Thunder. "You must have important business to take you there. Lomaki has been abandoned since the winter solstice." He paused, letting his words settle in every heart. "Youth is sometimes more courageous than wise, but I, for one, admire your courage. You must be very brave indeed to go to a haunted village where others have left in terror."

Walker's skin crawled listening to the man. Silent Thunder was slick—slick like a snake. Was he also dangerous?

"Great Owl, I know that your grandfather's people built Lomaki, but what Silent Thunder says is true." Leaning Tree's voice was low. "On the longest night of the winter, the few remaining people left Lomaki."

Silent Thunder spoke to Walker's men. "They vanished in the middle of the night. No one knows why they left, but there had been strange and frightening happenings at Lomaki for many moons."

Whatever Silent Thunder's game was, fear, intimidation, and superstition were the rules. Anger flared in Walker. He had faced bullies before, but never one so skilled.

"Strange things happen no matter where one goes. These happenings usually have very simple causes," Walker delivered his words directly to Silent Thunder. "My people need a place to live until we are ready to go on. We have no desire to be a burden on any village. We are capable and willing to provide for ourselves. All we seek is a place to stay in peace and harmony. Lomaki is Great Owl's ancestral home. The spirits of his forefathers will welcome and protect us there."

Silent Thunder's dark eyes were an open challenge to Walker's words. "You have been warned. The blood of your people will be on your hands."

# 4

A dust devil swirled toward the small band of people. Walker stared at the funnel-shaped cloud that was taller than he was. He heard startled gasps behind him as the others saw the whirlwind.

"A spirit cloud." Small Cub voiced the fear that Walker knew each heart felt.

As if it had heard the words, the circular wind veered. Sweeping up black dust from the cinder-covered ground, it whirled toward the abandoned two-story dwelling that stood strong against the harsh blue sky. Walker held his breath as the dust devil did a wild, swirling dance in front of the only entrance into Lomaki. In a heartbeat, it entered the low, T-shaped door, paused for a second as if to dare anyone to follow, and then disappeared from sight within the walls of the pueblo.

"A sign, it's a sign."

"What they said is true."

"Lomaki is haunted!"

Was it a sign? No, it was just a desert wind, Walker's twentieth-century mind told him, but superstition echoed in his heart with each rapid beat.

"It is a sign." Walker forced his voice to sound confident. He saw fear and apprehension, even on the faces of Flute Maiden and Son of Great Bear. White Badger stared at Lomaki with uncertain curiosity. Walker felt Great Owl's penetrating eyes upon him. He found support within the seer's eyes but realized that again Great Owl expected him to assume leadership and handle the situation.

*This is ridiculous! Great Owl knows that Lomaki isn't haunted. Why doesn't he just say so?* Walker took his frustration out in long strides toward Lomaki. He touched the red Moenkopi sandstone wall. It was warm. Walker prayed loudly, "Taawa, bless this house that we might stay here in peace."

He bent down and went inside the T-shaped door. A dusty, unused smell met his nose. Cool air filled his lungs. The morning light streamed into the small entrance room through two narrow, rectangular windows. The unplastered room was empty except for a two-inch-thick stone slab used to barricade the door and a large, black basalt metate with rounded sides. In the porous grinding stone's deep trough was a loaf-shaped, two-handed grinding stone, called a mano. The hard-packed dirt floor was carpeted with hundreds of jagged pieces of pottery. Walker was amazed at the various colors— white, brown, red, and gray. Some of the shards had designs. The most common combinations seemed to be white with black designs and red with black designs.

White Badger crawled through the door. He studied the anteroom and ran his fingers across the front wall. "This is a beautiful house. I have never seen such skillful workmanship. Each stone slab is cut to the same size and shape. The people must have had a very good reason to leave. This village was built to last many generations."

A cold shiver spread across Walker's shoulders as the haunting image of the lonely and desolate Lomaki Ruin of the 1990s flashed through his mind. He felt hollow inside as he gazed at the strong walls surrounding him. Yes, Lomaki would stand for hundreds of years, but could his people survive here even for a few short weeks? For the first time Walker began to doubt his decision to stay here. Maybe they should just push ahead to Hopi and take their chance to make it with what little food they had.

"Let's see what the rest looks like," White Badger said, stooping to go through the only inside doorway.

Walker and White Badger worked their way through the maze of small rooms on the ground level. Each wall was plastered with a smooth, neat coat of mud. Stone-lined fire pits, with ashes still in them, stood in the center of each of the larger chambers. The smaller, adjoining rooms appeared to be storage areas. Each room lay empty except for the pottery shards strewn on the floors.

A log ladder in the center room led up to the second story. As Walker climbed the worn, smooth ladder, he noted the fine workmanship of the ceiling with its huge log beams. Grass and brush were tightly matted between the beams to insulate the rooms from both the heat and cold. He had stared up at just such a ceiling every night before he went to sleep in Náat's house at Hopi. How many times had Náat told him the story of the huge beams? Walker could almost hear Náat's strong voice recounting the tale that his great-grandfather had recited to him. Walker knew that each beam in the village had been dragged ninety miles across the desert from the San Francisco Peaks, which his people called *Nuvatukya'ovi*. Walker felt sure that the beams here at Lomaki had also come from the sacred mountain.

The second-floor rooms were also like a maze, and a single ladder led up to the roof. Small windows let the bright sunlight stream into the larger chambers, but the light did little to eradicate the oppressive feeling that filled the walls of Lomaki.

"There is enough room for everyone," White Badger said, climbing off the ladder onto the roof. "It is almost like it was built for us."

Walker looked around the littered rooftop. "This was a work area." Three large metates stood in one corner. Two of the heavy grinding stones were flat, rectangular slabs of sandstone with worn furrows in their centers for grinding corn. The third metate was a thick, round stone with a deep, circular basin in the center. A smooth, round mona, used to grind and crush nuts and seed rested in the metate's basin.

Piles of woven yucca mats lay rotting in the sun. A long log-pole ladder that would reach the ground below lay half buried under one pile of mats near the roof's edge.

"We'll use it for sleeping, too." White Badger studied the vast landscape below. "It's the perfect place for someone keep watch."

Walker reached down and picked up a piece of broken pottery. The vivid black design swirled against a deep red background. Why would anyone shatter such a beautiful piece of work? Out of anger—spite?

"When we left the canyon, our women left their pottery

unbroken," Walker said, picking up another odd-shaped shard with an equally attractive design.

White Badger moved closer to Walker. "I was thinking the same thing. If these people left suddenly in the middle of the night, they wouldn't have been able to take much."

"We had a day to prepare, yet we left much more behind." Walker let the shards fall from his hand. "All there is here are the metates, which are too heavy to carry off, and shattered pottery."

White Badger's voice matched the suspicion in his eyes. "Perhaps someone knew Lomaki wasn't haunted and came here and stole everything."

"Walker, White Badger," Son of Great Bear's nervous voice called from below.

They moved to the edge of the roof. The people huddled together near the village entrance. Fear, uncertainty, and fatigue were written upon their uplifted faces. Walker called down, "Lomaki is a house of beauty. From this roof we will face the sacred mountain to offer our morning prayers. Each evening we shall look to the northeast to see the pink mesas far on the horizon, because it is there we will go as soon as possible."

Great Owl stood apart from the others. He leaned wearily upon his staff. His eyes stared at *Nuvatukya'ovi,* the sacred mountain. The look on the seer's face sent fear racing through Walker, leaving him shaking. Was Great Owl seeing his people's spirits leaving Lomaki to live at the home of the dead on the sacred mountain?

The bright sunlight faded around Walker as a vision of two rocky graves clouded his eyes.

# 5

By late afternoon, Lomaki was livable. Walker felt pride as he watched the women decide which room each family would use and set to work cleaning their temporary homes.

After being swept clean, the roof again became a work and sleeping area. "This is a perfect place for me to work," Arrow Maker said, settling down in the middle of the roof, "and be the village's eyes at the same time."

"We'll trust your keen eyes and as we do your sharp knives," Walker said, watching Arrow Maker use an deer antler to flake a piece of obsidian into a precise arrowhead.

A daily rotation system began with Son of Great Bear, Scar Cheek, and Quiet Wind shouldering the huge ceramic water jugs and going to the Little Colorado River, some ten miles away, for water. Rising Sun and the teenage boys went hunting. The younger boys scurried for wood, armed with their hunting sticks and hoping to bring back rabbits as well.

Lomaki perched on the edge of a deep, rocky crack in the

earth. Walker realized that if rain fell, the small wash would run with water. So he and White Badger began making stone check dams across the narrow ravine to catch the precious water.

"It is amazing how fast women put down roots and set up a home," White Badger said, lifting a rock up onto one of the knee-high dams. His strong back glittered with sweat.

Walker stretched his aching shoulders. "There is wisdom in women claiming ownership of the house. It is the Hopi way, too." He hoisted a rock onto the dam. "I hope the women don't get attached to Lomaki. I don't think we should stay here any longer than absolutely necessary."

"I agree. There are too many . . ."

"Walker, Uncle White Badger!" Small Cub shouted, running down the rocky path into the wash. "People are coming! Arrow Maker saw them from the roof. Grandfather says to hurry." Small Cub skidded to a stop beside Walker. "He looks worried."

Silent Thunder, Flute Maiden, and Great Owl stood near Lomaki's door. Two of Silent Thunder's overfed men stood near a dead antelope that lay on the ground. A boy of about eleven years squatted nearby. His willow-thin body was bare except for a grimy loincloth and a thick coat of dirt. He kept his eyes to the ground but listened intently. Something about the boy tore at Walker's heart. As he walked toward the village, Walker studied the boy. Who was he? Surely he wasn't Silent Thunder's son or he would be better fed.

The scrawny boy reached out and petted a scroungy black dog that lay at his feet. The dog's long tongue hung out as it panted. Through its matted fur, its ribs stood out as much as the boy's. As the boy petted the dog, Walker saw thick bands of scars on the boy's bony shoulders and back. Walker's stomach twisted. Was this the way Silent Thunder treated his people?

"Your healing skill is well known, but no one told me of your great beauty," Silent Thunder said to Flute Maiden, who kept her eyes cast downward.

"Welcome to Lomaki." Walker fought to keep the anger from his voice as he stepped up and met Silent Thunder's glare. Something passed through the man's eye. Amusement? Disgust? Holding eye contact, Walker said, "We did not expect visitors so soon."

Silent Thunder turned to White Badger, now standing next to Great Owl, whose eyes warned caution. "I apologize for coming uninvited. I thought your people needed meat."

"We are very grateful. I hope that we may repay your kindness by sharing a meal with you," Flute Maiden answered before Walker could respond.

"I would like that," Silent Thunder spoke as if he and Flute Maiden were alone. "But my men are afraid to stay since so many strange things have happened here."

Walker saw no fear or uneasiness in the men, but the boy squirmed at Silent Thunder's words.

"I am surprised that such strong men frighten so easily," White Badger's voice had a sharp edge. Great Owl reached out and touched his son's arm.

"Physical strength is like a dry blade of grass when pitted against evil spirits." Silent Thunder's words were spoken loud enough for the women watching from the roof to hear. He leaned closer to Flute Maiden, brushing his shoulder against hers. "If you need anything, just send word to my village. I know we will see much of each other." He turned to leave.

The boy sprang up so fast that he bumped into Flute

Maiden, almost knocking her over. Silent Thunder whirled around and knocked the boy to the ground, only to seize him by the hair and pull him to his feet again.

"It was nothing," cried Flute Maiden as both Walker and White Badger lunged forward to help the boy.

Silent Thunder released his hold. "No Name is a rude and stupid child!"

"He looks like a hungry child." Walker kept his voice even.

"He eats more than he works."

"Then leave him with me."

Silent Thunder's hard eyes glared at Walker. "He is mine. But you may have his worthless dog. It may come in handy when the meat runs out."

"No!" the boy flew at Silent Thunder. "You can't give my . . ."

Silent Thunder struck him in the face, knocking him to the ground.

Walker sprung in and stood inches from Silent Thunder, who was three inches taller and twenty pounds heavier. "I do not know what manners you use at your village, but I won't have you hurting *anyone* at my village."

Silent Thunder turned his back on Walker. "Get the boy," he snarled to his men.

The men lifted No Name to his feet and dragged him along. "Take care of Dog," the boy looked up at Walker and pleaded as they passed.

Walker saw worry and grief in the boy's face, but something else burned in the dark eyes—enormous determination and strength.

\* \* \*

The night air was still. Walker shifted on his sleeping mat and looked up at the bright stars in the black velvet sky. How could such ugliness exist in the same sphere as such beauty, he wondered, thinking about Silent Thunder.

Dog, lying next to him, raised its head and sniffed the air. "It's okay." Walker rubbed her head. Dog had tried to follow the boy. Walker had tied a yucca rope around her to keep her from leaving. At first Dog seemed wary of his kindness. Walker kept her by his side all day, sharing his food with her.

Now Dog seemed to accept Walker and his ways. Walker scratched her ear. "I know you miss your master." Dog looked at him with sad eyes and laid her head on his chest.

Walker's thoughts went around in circles—No Name, Dog, Silent Thunder, Flute Maiden. How could Flute Maiden be so civil to that man?

Easy. She was kind and courteous to everyone; it was her nature. Flute Maiden had seen the man's cruelty. Surely she was smart enough to see past the handsome face and smooth words.

An uneasiness took over Walker. Yes, Flute Maiden was wise enough to judge for herself, yet how many men had paid attention to her before? Did she have enough experience with men to be able to see them clearly, especially one as handsome and cunning as Silent Thunder?

Heat raced through Walker. Was he jealous of Silent Thunder, threatened by his good looks and his attention to Flute Maiden? Suddenly Walker wondered if *he* were seeing the situation clearly or through a veil of jealousy.

*What right do I have to be jealous? I have no claim on Flute Maiden.* Every minute of the day was spent on being high chief. The weight of his people lay so heavy on him that he couldn't even think about the responsibility of a wife. Besides, he wasn't even sure if Flute Maiden wanted to become his companion. He had nothing to offer her, absolutely nothing.

Walker closed his eyes against the darkness, confusion, and pain. He let sleep draw him into its safe shelter.

Hours later, Dog's growling brought Walker out of his restless sleep. Walker sat up. An eerie tinkling sound echoed through the blackness. It was answered by moaning from within the rocks below Lomaki. Dog growled louder but still didn't bark.

The hair on Walker's neck stood on end.

# 6

A long, wailing howl filled the cool night air. Goose bumps covered Walker's body. Dog rushed to the edge of the roof. Growling, she stood staring down into the moonlit darkness. Walker struggled to his feet, trying to throw off his sleepiness and fear.

White Badger moved on his sleeping mat a couple of feet away. The echo of the wail died, but the hollow, tinkling sound sang through the darkness. Walker knelt beside Dog. Her growls became more intense as the sound drew closer.

"What is it?" White Badger crouched beside Walker.

"Not what, *who*?"

Dog's growling turned into furious barking.

"Let's go find our evil spirits." Walker lowered the long log pole ladder over the side of the roof.

White Badger followed as Walker carried Dog down the ladder. As they descended, Walker heard ghostly moans coming from the west. The sound seemed human—*or did it?*

As Walker's foot hit the ground, something deathly cold touched his shoulder. He jolted around, his heart in his throat. As pale as a ghost, Great Owl stood there.

Great Owl's voice was a breathless whisper. "Evil is close by." His old body trembled as he turned to White Badger, who was stepping off the ladder. "You must be careful."

From somewhere nearby came the hollow bell sound. Dog leaped out of Walker's arms and disappeared into the darkness. Walker and White Badger followed.

The loose cinders slipped under Walker's yucca sandals. He fought to keep on his feet as he followed the barking. White Badger was two steps behind him. The bright moonlight draped each cactus, rock, mound, and butte in a flat, grayish light that cast haunting shadows.

Dog's barking echoed against the surrounding cinder hills but sounded more to the north now than before. The barking suddenly turned into a sharp yelp of pain.

Walker jerked to a stop and listened. The sounds of movement through cinders came from the south. Drawing out his stone knife, Walker started toward the sound. The crunching noise came closer. Walker's scalp tightened.

Dog limped into sight and cowered on her belly with a whine.

"It's okay, girl." Walker bent and petted her. She yelped.

White Badger was at Walker's shoulder. "What is it?"

"One of the spirits kicked Dog hard enough to break a rib."

\* \* \*

"Evil spirits do not leave sandal prints." The midmorning sun beat down upon Walker, yet an unnatural coldness pumped through his body.

"He is right," said White Badger. "Only men could have made the foot marks we found this morning." The people were gathered on the roof to discuss the frightening events of their first night at Lomaki.

Walker looked over at Great Owl. The seer's face was unreadable. When Walker and White Badger had sought him out earlier in the morning for advice, Great Owl said, "The journey to Hopi will be long and difficult. Life at Lomaki will be short and difficult. You as high chief and warrior chief must make the decisions." He peered at Walker and stated with firmness, "You must use your inner sight. My eyes are growing cloudy, my powers weak." Now Great Owl sat apart from the group, watching, listening, but saying nothing.

"A boy at Strong House told me that the children here disappeared one at a time," Small Cub said, his eyes round with fear. "Evil spirits stole them away."

"Many of the men died in their fields," Fawn added, cradling her son closer.

"We'll stay in pairs wherever we go. The children must stay close to the village and always in a group." Walker saw a few heads nod in agreement. "Guards will be posted on the roof each night. Dog will let us know if anyone is close."

White Badger added, "If we are to survive the long journey to Hopi, we must have more provisions."

A tense silence, rippled with fear, filled the group.

"Certain plants and herbs grow here that I need for medicines." Flute Maiden held Walker's eyes for an instant then looked toward the others. "I am not sure I can get them at Hopi. It won't take long to gather them."

The uncomfortable silence continued. Walker knew each person was waiting for his final decision. He took a deep breath and prayed it was the correct one. "I have no desire to stay here any longer than necessary. Together we will work hard for what we will need and leave Lomaki as soon as possible." He saw uncertainty in most eyes. "See with your hearts. Lomaki is not haunted by evil spirits. It is here to shelter and protect us until we are ready to go on."

A high, billowing cloud glided across the sun's bright rays, casting Lomaki in a dark shadow.

\* \* \*

"Son of Great Bear, Rising Sun, and I are ready to leave for water," White Badger called up from the ground. He and the others had a water jug slung over each shoulder.

Walker looked down at the men from the roof of Lomaki. "The long hike is worth a bath in the river. It's my turn tomorrow." He and Scar Cheek were staying at Lomaki while the others went for water or hunted. "Taawa be with you. Leave some water in the river for me to wash in," Walker called and watched until the three men disappeared down off the plateau that Lomaki was built upon. If only there was a water source closer for us to use, thought Walker, it would be so much easier. *It's only for a few weeks at the most.* He wiped the sweat off his forehead and turned to survey the rooftop.

Arrow Maker had already taken his post in the center of the roof and was busy flaking a large piece of obsidian. Early Snow sat nearby cutting long strips of the antelope meat to dry in the sun for jerky. She visited in hushed, nervous tones with Gray Dove, who was scraping the hair from the antelope hide with a stone.

47

Walker knelt beside Arrow Maker. "I think it would be good to start bartering with the other villages as soon as possible so we can get what we need."

"When I finish this knife, I'll start making spearheads. I can make them faster and they will bring just as much in return." The obsidian in Arrow Maker's hand caught the sun's glint. "We will need to get more stone. There is a special place on the sacred mountain where a suitable stone is found. My son, Fast Lizard, knows where to find it."

"White Badger and I will see that you have all the stone you need. The more we can trade for, the sooner we will be able to leave."

"I can make small pouches from this hide," Gray Dove said in a low voice, without looking up from her tedious work. "Perhaps Flute Maiden could fill them with tea or medicines to barter."

"I know just the kinds of tea that people will want," Flute Maiden said walking toward the group. She carried a large basket over her slender shoulder. Her shiny black hair flowed to her narrow waist.

Walker hadn't seen her come up the ladder. In fact, he hadn't seen her much since the incident with Silent Thunder yesterday. The surge of uneasiness he felt vanished when he saw her warm smile. Flute Maiden stood above Gray Dove and touched her shoulder. "I was just hunting for Small Cub to go with me to gather plants and herbs. I will gather extra for your pouches."

"It would be better to take one of the older boys instead," Walker said, standing up next to Flute Maiden.

She looked up at him. "I won't go far today. Maybe tomorrow you could come with me and we can go further."

"It is my turn to go for water," Walker stammered, feeling his face turn red.

Flute Maiden nodded, and her smile seemed to get tight. "Of course. I understand."

* * *

When dusk fell, the thick slab of rock was slid across the entrance of Lomaki and the two-story pole ladder pulled up to the roof. Walker and Son of Great Bear took the night's first watch. Walker searched the sky. Thick, rainless clouds hid the moon and stars, making it almost impossible to see more than a few feet.

"I doubt we'll have any visitors tonight," Walker said peering into the blackness. "Without the moonlight it will be difficult for anyone to see where he is going without a torch, even if it is to cause trouble."

Son of Great Bear whispered back, "Spirits need no light to see by."

The statement startled Walker, sending a snake of cold up his back. Did Son of Great Bear, so logical, practical, and brave, really believe that evil spirits haunted Lomaki? Could he possibly be right? A prickling sensation spread across Walker's shoulders as he peered uneasily into the blackness.

"S trange that *evil spirits* are frightened off by such a small dog," Walker said the next morning after a peaceful night. The rocky landscape was tinted in a grayish, pre-dawn light as he, Quiet Wind, and Scar Cheek left Lomaki to get water.

He turned his head and looked over the water jugs on his shoulders to the ghostly silhouette of Lomaki. If only Great Owl would tell me what lies in the days ahead, Walker thought, then turned his eyes forward to the rocky path ahead of him. The empty water jugs bounced heavily on his shoulder, sharp cinders slipped into his sandals, and weariness cut into his soul. Was the future so bleak, so frightening, that even Great Owl refused to see it?

"The fields I passed while hunting yesterday had the same kind of shelter built at their edges," Quiet Wind said as the three men passed a square, one-room rock-and-mud dwelling. High weeds growing in its low northeast doorway testified to long abandonment.

Scar Cheek responded, "Farmers must have stayed in them during the growing season, guarding the fields day and night to keep the rats, mice, rabbits, and birds from eating the plants."

Walker studied the large field they were passing. Long rock walls, one rock deep and one or two rocks high, ran parallel to the slope of the hill. He could tell that the crops had been planted between the walls so they would reap the benefit of any water runoff. The walls would serve as windbreaks as well, Walker thought, as he moved along. The steep slope to the east had been terraced in neat rows, also for catching water.

"There are abandoned fields to the south of Lomaki, where the farmers planted like we do." Beneath Quiet Wind's straight bangs, his dark eyes reflected his farming interest and experience. "I could see where the corn, beans, pumpkins, and squash had been planted with big water catches around each one." He pointed with his chin to a neat stack of stones they were passing. "Those fields had the same pyramid-shaped piles of stone around their edges."

"The Hopi clans mark the boundaries of each of their fields with special stone markers called Qalalni," Walker told them.

"A good many fields are planted in the higher places, on the hills and butte tops," Quiet Wind commented, shifting the jugs on his shoulders.

"I've noticed that, too," Walker said, stopping. A small cinder had wedged itself between his toes and the thick mat of plaited yucca fibers that made up his sandal. The two men stopped beside him and rested while Walker untied the long yucca straps that wrapped over the top of his foot and around his ankle. "They probably have to plant in the higher place where it is warmer, since the growing season here is short." Walker picked out the small, sharp pebble that had embedded itself in the yucca plait. He wished that he had kept his jogging shoes instead of sending them with Tag. They were too small for Tag's huge, stumbling feet, but the white leather hightops would have brought too many stares and questions here. An idea formulated in Walker's mind as he retied the yucca strap around his ankle. With Scar Cheek's sandal-making skill and Quiet Wind's moccasin-making knowledge, perhaps the three of them together could come up with footwear that would be more practical and durable than the yucca sandals that shredded so easily in the knife-sharp cinders.

As they started down the path again, Scar Cheek said, "As a boy, I remember hearing my father talk about this great area. He said there were so many villages full of people that they dug huge reservoirs to catch water in order to quench everyone's thirst." He shook his head as his strong legs scissored down the path. "Even that didn't work, judging by the number of abandoned fields and villages I have seen already."

Vivid apparitions of the future flashed through Walker's mind. A narrow asphalt ribbon cut through the cinder hills, connecting the hollow, windswept ruins. Long, shiny, air-conditioned buses, packed with pale-skinned people carrying video cameras, belched diesel exhaust in the clean desert air. A steady stream of brightly colored cars zoomed in and around the buses like busy ants, hurrying to the next incredible ruin, speeding to the most picturesque view point, and finally racing to the Park Service Visitor Center with its cold soda machine and flushing toilets.

"Three distinct Indian cultures: the Sinagua, the Kayenta

Anasazi, and the Cohonina, all lived in the Wupatki area from approximately A.D. 1066 to the mid 1200s. *Having three different cultures living in such close proximity makes Wupatki National Monument an unusual place."* Walker heard in his mind the memorized words of the overly tanned bahana woman in a Smoky the Bear hat and gray Park Service shirt. *"At its zenith, this area supported an estimated population of more than two thousand men, women, and children. The Wupatki area was a major trade center in the Southwest . . ."*

"Trade is the only thing that keeps this place alive." Quiet Wind's voice interrupted Walker's memory of the future, bringing his eyes and mind back to the scorching sun and the heavy jugs swinging on his shoulders.

"I doubt even trade can support what few villages are left for many more seasons if the drought doesn't end very soon," stated Scar Cheek, kicking up a cloud of fine cinder dust with his sandal.

Walker's head pounded. He tried to swallow the tightness in his throat, but his mouth was too dry.

\* \* \*

Smoke rose in thin, airy streams from Lomaki as Walker, straining under the weight of the full water jugs, crested the final hill. Sweat ran down his back in rivulets but quickly dried in the late afternoon wind. The thick leather straps on the jugs bit into his tired shoulders with each step. Seeing Lomaki, Walker felt relief edged with apprehension. Was everything as they had left it? he worried, picking up his pace.

A small figure stood on Lomaki's roof. It began jumping around, pointing in Walker's direction. Small Cub's anxious shouts carried in the wind. "There they are! I see them

53

coming! White Badger, they are coming!" The sound of Small Cub's voice sent a shiver up Walker's back.

Women gathered around Small Cub in a tight cluster on the roof. Walker sensed their fear as he hurried forward. White Badger and Son of Great Bear, with faces drawn in anxiety, met Walker and the others a few hundred yards from Lomaki. White Badger reached for one of the jugs on Walker's shoulder. "Rising Sun is injured," he said, placing the jug on his own shoulder and falling in step with Walker.

"Flute Maiden and Arrow Maker's oldest son, Fast Lizard, went plant gathering again. She said they would be back before the sun was high, but they haven't returned yet. I was just going to hunt for them," Son of Great Bear said, his normally calm voice sounding distraught.

"I will go with you."

"Great Owl needs you." White Badger sounded strange. They were a few feet from the village door. He took the last jug from Walker. "He is with Rising Sun. I'll go with Son of Great Bear."

Rising Sun's pain-twisted face was pale against the fading light that streamed through the small, westerly window. Great Owl crouched beside him on one side. Fawn knelt on the ground on the opposite side. Both looked up anxiously as Walker entered. He squatted down beside Great Owl, who held a piece of blood-soaked cloth on Rising Sun's thigh.

Great Owl's face was streaked with sweat and fatigue. "He has lost a great deal of blood, but the bleeding has finally stopped. The wound is gaping. His ankle is not broken but is badly twisted." Worry radiated from Great Owl's dark eyes, sunken deep in his weary face. "Flute Maiden isn't back yet. She should have been back long ago."

"White Badger and Son of Great Bear are going to find her." Walker studied Rising Sun. His chest and legs were a mass of crisscrossed abrasions. His left ankle was swollen to twice its size and was an angry red. Ignoring politeness, Walker asked, "What happened?"

"I fell," Rising Sun said through gritted teeth. "I was climbing the cinder hill to the east, hunting. My foot slipped between the rocks, and one of them rolled onto my ankle." His voice broke off in pain.

Fawn held her husband's hand. "His knife somehow slashed his leg as he fell. He managed to get partway back on his own but fell many times before anyone heard his calls."

"We need to get his ankle elevated to help keep the swelling down," Walker instructed, wishing there was ice or even cool water to put on the ankle. Walker glanced at Great Owl, who suddenly looked like a weathered twig fluttering in a strong wind. His entire body shook in a rhythmic spasm.

"Great Owl," Walker cried, reaching out to steady him. The seer's brittle skin felt like it was on fire. Great Owl's weight fell against Walker. "Fawn, go get Morning Flower. Hurry!" He eased Great Owl down beside Rising Sun. "Bring one of the jugs of water we just brought in," Walker called after her.

"Your sight—you must use it," Great Owl whispered, staring up at Walker. "You must keep your heart free from anger and hate so that you *can see*." He squeezed Walker's hand tightly. "Use your sight to see Flute Maiden's heart before it is too late!"

# 8

"Where have you been?" All of Walker's self-control vanished. The sound of his voice amplified the worry, fear, and frustration he now felt in the darkest hours of the night.

The swaying torchlight cast harsh shadows across Flute Maiden's face as she knelt beside Great Owl opposite Walker. She felt Great Owl's forehead and laid her ear on his chest, listening. Raising her head she said, "Morning Flower, I need more water, and please have someone get the basket of plants that I brought back with me. It's in the entry room."

"I wasn't sure what to do," Morning Flower said, rubbing her hands together. "I gave Father some of the tea you use when the babies are too hot, but he couldn't drink very much."

Flute Maiden nodded, opening her medicine bag, which was made from a small fox pelt. "You did just what you should have. Please go get water and the basket. I need some of the plants in it for medicine." She gave her sister a weak smile. "I think Father will be all right."

A strained silence filled the room. Walker fought to get his anger under control as he watched Flute Maiden open a leather drawstring pouch and pour some of its content into a white ceramic bowl. She kept her eyes down, her jaw muscles pulled tight. "Has he opened his eyes or spoken?"

"He has been mumbling things all night; most of it was incoherent. Just before you got here, he called your name a few times." Walker noticed a stunning turquoise ring on Flute Maiden's finger as she worked. It was a small, delicate version of a ring Silent Thunder wore. "Where were you?"

Flute Maiden glanced at him, coldness in her eyes. "On my way back from gathering plants, I met two men from Leaning Tree's village. They were on their way to get me. One of their women was having a very difficult birth." She searched her fox bag for another drawstring pouch. Finding it, she pulled it out; the silver of her ring caught the torch's light. "I went to assist."

"You were needed here!"

Flute Maiden stared at Walker. "I didn't know."

"You should have sent Fast Lizard to tell us where you were," Walker fired back.

"I didn't feel it was safe to have him come back alone."

Great Owl moaned and turned his gaunt face toward Walker. His sunken eyes struggled to focus.

"I am here, Father," Flute Maiden said, smoothing a strand of white hair out of his face. "Everything is going to be all right."

Great Owl's eyes penetrated Walker's. "Use your sight," he whispered. "See her heart." He closed his eyes mumbling, "See her heart."

White Badger crawled through the low doorway with

Flute Maiden's large shoulder basket and knelt beside their father, cradling his hand. He looked at Flute Maiden, questioning. Physical fatigue hung on both of them like heavy water jugs. Flute Maiden reached for the basket. Her shoulders sagged. Her voice shook, "I'm not sure . . ."

"I know," White Badger said. "You'll do the best you can. I'll stay and help."

Walker shifted, feeling embarrassed and ashamed. It wasn't Flute Maiden's fault her father was sick or that Rising Sun lay injured in the next room. Just as it wasn't his fault, either. Or was it? his exhausted mind questioned. If they had gone straight to Hopi instead of staying here at Lomaki, none of this would have happened.

Yet, hadn't Great Owl said that they should stay at Lomaki? Walker tried to remember, his mind was thick with fatigue. No, but Great Owl had indicated it, hadn't he? Well, there was no choice now. Until Great Owl and Rising Sun could travel, they would have to stay.

"I'm going to go check on Rising Sun," Walker blurted out, rushing to his feet. He had to get away—away from Flute Maiden, Great Owl, and his own inner turmoil.

\* \* \*

"It will be many days before Rising Sun is able to travel," White Badger said, standing next to Walker on the roof hours later. A brilliant sunset now blazed across the western sky. "Flute Maiden thinks that some of his ankle muscles are torn. She said the cut on his leg should heal, though, as long as evil spirits don't enter it. I just can't understand how his own knife could have done such damage when he fell. It just isn't logical."

"Great Owl," Walker made it a statement, not a question. Too ashamed, he had not been back to see Great Owl since the ugly scene with Flute Maiden, but had stayed with Rising Sun until Flute Maiden came to care for him. Walker left the room without a word. Now after many hours, the anger in his heart was gone.

White Badger sank down onto his sleeping mat. He put his face into his hands, shook his head, and mumbled, "Flute Maiden doesn't know." He peered up. "I'm afraid, Walker. I'm afraid he is going . . ."

Walker didn't hear his friend. The stark, cold vision of two rocky graves, side by side, burst into his mind, blocking out White Badger's words.

\* \* \*

The late autumn morning air was crisp. Finishing his morning prayer on the rooftop, Walker opened his eyes and spit over his right shoulder for his daily cleansing. The first rays of the sun were spreading thin fingers of life down the tall cinder hill to the east. Walker pulled the turkey feather blanket around his bare shoulders. The cold of winter was drawing closer. The ever-present desire to leave Lomaki burned in Walker's chest. *If only we could leave today, tomorrow, or even next week. If only Great Owl* . . . Walker sighed, pushing the thoughts to the back of his mind as he had done hundreds of time during the last three months.

He shifted to a cross-legged position. Dog thumped her tail against the roof and peered up from where she lay. Walker scratched her ear. "One more quiet night passed. Let's hope the day is as quiet." On only a few nights had the haunting sounds disrupted Lomaki's sleep. Dog's barking had frightened the sounds away, but each night the rock slab stood strong at Lomaki's entrance. By day the people were cautious as they worked, falling into the security of daily routines and patterns, but Walker knew that many looked over their shoulders with fear.

Walker turned his face to the rising sun, letting its warmth bathe his face. He closed his eyes and let the vivid memories of the past three months become a kaleidoscope of sights, sounds, and feelings within his mind.

Rising Sun's thigh wound was slow to heal, and his ankle was even slower. "I feel so worthless—just sitting around not hunting," he had told Walker.

"But you're not just sitting," Walker responded. They had been on the roof in the cool of evening. Walker was watching Rising Sun carve, trying to learn some of his artistic techniques. "We barter everything you make for food. You can't make hair barrettes, combs, or weaving tools fast enough. People are now even coming here to trade instead of us having to travel to their villages."

Small chips of wood flew around Rising Sun's square hands. "Life would be easier for the others if I could at least help with the water."

*Life here will never be easy.* Walker had kept the thought to himself.

The memories of many hours spent talking, planning, discussing, and working with White Badger drifted through Walker's mind, like the warmth of the sun. He realized again how fortunate he was to have White Badger as warrior chief and close friend. One memory kept playing itself through Walker's mind. They were at the Little Colorado River filling the water jugs. *Little* was the only part of the future name that fit the small stream of water working its way through the bottom of a deep, rugged gorge.

"How many days of actual walking will it take to get from Lomaki to the Hopi mesas?" White Badger was standing calf-deep in the slow-moving water.

Walker pulled off his worn sandals and thrust his feet into the shallow flow. The icy water bit at his sweaty feet. He was glad that their close relationship allowed them to ask direct questions without being considered rude. It made communication more precise and clear. "It's hard to say, since I have never actually traveled it on foot." Walker saw White Badger's eyes widen a bit. Despite their open friendship, Walker never tried to explain or describe to his friend what life was like in the future. It was beyond White Badger's experiences or imagination. Even Walker himself had a hard time remembering and accepting what life would be like in seven hundred years. "I am sure it will take more than a full moon cycle, since we don't move very fast as a group."

"I hope the maidens at Hopi are worth such a long walk," White Badger joked, splashing water over his strong chest and rubbing the dirt off.

Walker knew that despite the open flirting from many of the beautiful maidens in other villages, White Badger felt the same obligation that he did. He was not free to think about the responsibility of taking a wife until his people were settled at Hopi.

"From what I remember they are, and their mothers have fine houses, too. Their tradition is like ours. After marrying, men live in their mother-in-law's house." Walker dunked his head down under the water to wash his hair. It felt wonderful to be clean, even if only temporarily. By the time he had hauled the heavy water jugs back to Lomaki, he would be sweaty and dirty again.

"We can't leave Lomaki too soon," White Badger said as he retied his loincloth. "I have a gut feeling that there is much more going on in this area than the other villages have let us see."

Walker pulled on his sandals and lifted one of the water jugs onto his wet shoulder. "It is good to know that I'm not the only one who feels that way."

"Whatever is going on, Silent Thunder is a big part of it, and I don't want our people involved in any of it," White Badger stated. With water jugs on each shoulder, he had started up the narrow path leading out of the gorge.

Walker's mind shifted, recalling scenes from the last three months, and focused on a pleasant memory. His stomach had growled as he watched Small Cub proudly skinning the rabbit he had just killed. "I'm a true man now," Small Cub declared, working the skin away from the underfed animal.

"Oh-ay, yes, you are. We must have your hunting initiation before the moon cycle is out," Son of Great Bear answered, pride gleaming in his face. "Hold the knife a little closer. That's the way. We will be able to loosen our belts a little now that you are a such a good hunter."

But belts remained cinched tight. The struggle for food never ended, even with every available man and boy hunting antelope, deer, rabbit, prairie dogs, and even ground squirrels. The women gathered everything edible—pinion nuts, sunflower seeds, acorns, cactus fruits, wild tomatoes, and many other kinds of plants and roots. The larger part of their staples, corn, squash, beans, and pumpkins, came from bartering Fawn's pottery, Arrow Maker's spearheads and knives, Rising Sun's carvings, Littlest Star's baskets, Gray Dove's leatherwork, and Flute Maiden's medicines, teas, and medical services.

*Flute Maiden* . . . Walker winced, shattering the memories playing through his thoughts and feelings. He didn't have the emotional strength to relive the many tense, confusing, and painful moments he had shared with Flute Maiden since the day Rising Sun was injured. A quiet wall had begun to rise between them that day. Day by day, incident by incident, the invisible wall seemed to get higher—stronger, mortared tightly by the struggle for survival, worry, misunderstandings, poor communication, pride, and jealousy.

Walker was emotionally and physically drained by the demands and worries of daily leadership. He couldn't offer what Flute Maiden seemed to need and want in her aloof distance. Flute Maiden, too, was pushed beyond her limits by the health concerns of others. She spent much of her time at other villages delivering babies and administering to the sick. When at Lomaki, she was with Great Owl, nursing him physically and spiritually. He had never fully recovered from his mysterious sickness, which Walker heard people of the other villages whisper was spirit sickness.

The emotional wall between them had risen heart-high now. Too high for either of them to climb over, Walker thought with a wrenching ache.

The autumn sun now warmed Lomaki. The sounds of voices and movement in the rooms below brought Walker's attention back to the present. The others would be coming up to the roof to say their morning prayers—prayers that were the same as his daily petitions for peace, health, and enough food to eat.

Walker pulled on his leather shirt, leggings, and moccasins. Whether he was ready or not, it was time to face another day. Father Sun had begun his journey across the sky and would carry no one on his back.

Small Cub appeared on the ladder and ran over to Walker. "Father says that I must stay behind today, but I want to go to trade at Tall House, too." He looked up at Walker with hopeful eyes. "If you talk to him, I know he will let me go."

"We must leave men here to help protect the women and children." The answer didn't satisfy Small Cub. Walker reached out and touched his shoulder. "I need someone here who will care for Dog, someone she obeys and I trust."

Small Cub's chest puffed out under his shell pendant. "Like me. I'll take care of Dog and sleep with her here on the roof."

"I know that Scar Cheek will want you to help guard since he and Rising Sun will be the only other men staying." Even as he said this, Walker again questioned his own judgment of leaving so few men behind while the others went to trade. Traders from hundreds of miles away would be at Tall House for the last big gathering before the snow. If things went well trading, they would be finally ready to leave for Hopi at last. *That is, if Great Owl can . . .*

Small Cub interrupted Walker's thoughts. "I'll go talk to Scar Cheek right now and ask if I can sleep here on the roof. Come on, Dog." The two scampered off.

"I hope Morning Flower approves of him sleeping up here," Flute Maiden's voice came from behind Walker. It had the distant quality he had come to dread.

Walker's heart quickened, but his stomach twisted. He

turned to face her. "The responsibility is good for him." Walker chose his words carefully but still felt the tension between them.

He noticed that she was wearing the delicate, red coral earrings that Silent Thunder had sent her yesterday. The dangling earrings were just one of Silent Thunder's many gifts to her. Each gift, hand-delivered by his men, was sent with an invitation for Flute Maiden to visit his village. She had never gone, but Walker knew that she had met Silent Thunder by chance at least twice at Strong House and once at another village. Walker had no idea what had taken place between them. His pride kept him from asking even White Badger, who didn't like or trust the man, either. Flute Maiden was the only topic that he and White Badger didn't discuss.

"Father seems stronger today," Flute Maiden said. "He'd like to have you and White Badger bring him up here before you and the others leave for Tall House."

"It sounds like you have decided not to go."

Flute Maiden fingered one of the coral earrings. She gazed at the horizon beyond with a faraway look. "There is too much uncertainty—here and there."

*Uncertainty with who? Silent Thunder or me?* Walker kept the words within his head.

"I'm so worried about Father." Her voice had the soft, musical quality that Walker loved but so seldom heard now. Flute Maiden's eyes clouded with tears. "He gets weaker each day. He has no pain, no sickness that I can see, yet his life's breath is slipping away. It is as if he is listening more to the spirits of his ancestors than he listens to . . ." Sobs choked her words.

Walker reached out and touched her shoulder. She didn't

pull away, so he gently put his arms around her. Walker felt her hot tears on his chest. When was the last time they had stood this close, let alone touched? Walker held her tight and tried to find words to comfort her, but none would come. What she said was true. Each day Great Owl grew more detached and physically weaker. He left all responsibility to Walker and White Badger. Even when they went to him for advice and counsel, Great Owl listened intently but had little to say except that he trusted them to make the right decisions. Had Great Owl decided not to leave the home of his ancestors? The thought sent a chill up Walker's back.

"Father told me to go to Tall House, that many there will need medicines and that he needs none." Flute Maiden pulled away from Walker. "Walker, I want to stay here with Father, but I want to go to be with . . ." She turned her face away but not before Walker saw her blush. "I'm afraid that if I don't go things will remain the same, but if I do go things will change between—"

*Between who?* Walker wanted to scream. But as so many times before, his tongue refused to utter the thoughts of his heart. Until he got the people safely settled at Hopi, he had no right to speak what was in his heart. Nor could he expect her to wait until he had finished what he had been sent back in time to do. She had every right to become someone's wife and have the children she so desperately wanted. Frustration and anger swept over Walker.

"The decision is yours." He felt her eyes burning on him as he walked toward the ladder.

# 9

Although the sun was high in the cloudless sky above the open amphitheater at Tall House, the air was crisp. The huge circular structure, used for social and religious gatherings, was thirty-five feet across with a large fire pit near the center. At the only entrance, the four-foot-thick stone wall was almost as tall as Walker. As the wall circled around, it rose to seven feet at its peak, then tapered off again as it curled back around to the narrow entrance.

Partway up the massive wall, a wide rock bench jutted out and followed the contour of the wall. Many traders used the spacious bench to display their merchandise. Shell jewelry, finely-crafted painted pottery, stone and wooden tools, and useful household goods were exhibited along with delicately carved wooden and bone hair ornaments, combs, buttons, and carved stone animal effigies. Turkey feathers or strips of rabbit skins woven together with yucca cordage made warm but lightweight blankets that were in high demand. Colorful cotton textiles fashioned into capes, tunics, skirts, or long kilts, decorated with shells, feathers, and beads brought high prices. Among the assortment of food, salt and dried fish seemed the most popular.

Walker's people and other less prestigious traders presented their wares on woven mats on the hard-packed ground in the center of the amphitheater. Yucca brooms and hairbrushes lay beside bone sewing awls, stone hoes, axes, and other tools. A large variety of footwear, including the sandals Scar Cheek had sent, drew many people. Small copper bells, shaped like sleigh bells of the future, were being bartered next to brightly colored, noisy parrots. Walker knew these had come all the way from what he knew as Mexico. He had seen parrots in some of the villages he had visited in the area and wondered if the birds were used in religious ceremonies. They didn't seem to be used as food.

Walker and White Badger stopped to inspect the large selection of cloud blowers, or ceremonial pipes, displayed by a distinguished-looking, older man with a pleasant smile and eager eyes. Many of the pipes were stubby and conical with tobacco bowls that made up almost a third of the length. Other pipes were straight tubes that tapered slightly from the bowl end to the stem. A good number of the pipes were decorated, but just as many were plain.

"As you see, I have the best choice of cloud blowers here," the distinguished merchant exclaimed. "I have whatever kind you prefer, clay, stone or even the scarce wooden cloud makers." He picked up a handsome, red clay pipe painted with a striking black rain cloud motif. "With the proper prayers, this cloud maker will blow clouds that will bring rain clouds so heavy that your corn plants will drink for an entire moon cycle." The trader set the pipe down. His enthusiastic eyes darted to small leather pouches arranged close by. "But of course, the tobacco you smoke is as important as the cloud blower itself. I have many different types of tobacco as well as exotic blends of tobacco, spices, and herbs that come from as far as the great water to the east. Each mixture has a rich taste and pleasing aroma. You are welcome to try any that you wish." His dark eyes snapped with alacrity.

"Kwa kwa for your generous offer," White Badger said, moving on, "maybe later."

Walker chuckled. Did White Badger know that the surgeon general of the United States would determine that smoking was harmful to your health? But then again, Walker thought, in A.D. 1200 something, almost everything is hazardous to your health.

The slim, foreign-looking trader offering small ceramic and wooden containers filled with paint pigments was busy. The colorful, crushed stone and mineral pigments were used for painting ceremonial objects and the body in certain sacred and social rites. These pigments would create a dazzling pallet of natural colors—shades of blue, gray, white, beige, red, brown-reds, yellow, orange, salmon, and ocher. Walker found himself wishing he knew which colors came from which kind of rock or mineral.

Inspecting the various goods, Walker was proud of the quality of his people's work. It was obvious that only the best quality or unusual items were being bartered. Many gathered around Arrow Maker, trading for his keen projectiles and knives. After the first day of trading, Fawn had only a few pieces of her graceful pottery left. Now, after two days, she had none, but she did have a good quantity of dried fish and cornmeal to take back to Lomaki. The others were also doing a brisk business. Even the simple bone flutes that Walker had carved were bartered for a few pinion nuts. The long day's journey hauling their goods from Lomaki to Tall House's marketplace had proven worth the effort.

Every minute of the two trading days had been busy for Walker's people. He had seen Flute Maiden only for a brief moment in the midst of the numerous health visits she was making, which had included delivering three babies. When he had caught a glimpse of her, she was standing near Silent Thunder, her face close to his. Walker cringed at the memory and forced his thoughts back to the amphitheater with its collage of people, sounds, and goods.

It's like the Indian Pow Wows of the future. I wish Tag were here to see everything, Walker thought, as he and White Badger threaded through the open-air market. "It is hard to believe so many have come so far to trade," he commented to White Badger.

"Fewer traders come each season, though. Father says when he was a boy, the game court down the hill overflowed with traders, too. Times are harder, leaner now." White Badger looked toward Tall House, rising three stories above them on a long, narrow rock ridge. "I wonder how many more winter moons will come before this huge village stands totally empty."

With a natural spring nearby, Tall House was the largest village in the area, capable of housing more than two hundred people. Many of the one hundred rooms within the long pueblo had been abandoned already. The cold finger of time reached out and pulled Walker's mind forward to 1993. Tall House, Wupatki Ruin, was nothing more than a massive mud-and-stone skeleton, crumbling against man and time. . .

A high-pitched screech brought Walker's mind back to the present. Nearby, a large green-and-yellow parrot was precariously perched on the shoulders of a dark-skinned, middle-aged man sitting on the stone bench. The bird cocked its head, scrutinizing Walker. Screeching, it scrambled back and forth along the length of the man's broad shoulders, keeping its beadlike eyes on Walker.

"Calm your loud voice, feathered one. You'll not frighten these two," the bird's owner said, his narrow, charcoal eyes examined Walker and White Badger. He had large ears that were out of portion with his small, round face. His long black hair rested on a bright cape that spoke of faraway lands. Displayed beside him on the stone bench was finely crafted shell jewelry—necklaces, bracelets, earrings, and pendants. Many items were cut into animal shapes and studded with turquoise or adorned with bright feathers. Other, simpler pieces achieved beauty with their distinctive, strong lines. The strange man openly inspected Walker. "You are the high chief of the people now living at Lomaki."

"Yes." Walker bent down and blew on the trader's open hand. It was soft and cool to the touch. "This is White Badger, our warrior chief."

White Badger blew on his hand as the man said, "You have your father's looks, but not his eyes." He turned his gaze back to Walker. "You are not Great Owl's son, yet you have his eyes." He paused, as if listening to something whispering to him. "But you have not accepted your inner sight. You must. It is gift that will not be denied."

Walker's shoulders tingled with coldness. He felt his face tighten.

"As a young boy, I met Great Owl here in this magnificent gathering place," the man continued in a deep voice. "Great Owl, the great magician and seer, spoke to me of my gift of hearing the shells' songs. He took the fear of listening from my mind and opened my soul."

Smiling, the man swept his arm over his shell jewelry. "I am Shell Listener. I know the treasures of the great waters as no other." He stared at White Badger and then back at Walker. "Each former inhabitant of the salty waters calls to me, whispering of the past and things yet to come." The bird chattered in a loud voice, adding his endorsement. "Even the shell pendant that hangs on your chest sings to me."

Walker reached up and touched his pendant.

"It recalls the father's loving hands that cut it into the shape of the eagle. As the father carved, he prayed that his wife of many years would be blessed with a son as brave as the eagle. The father inlaid the pendant with eighty-five pieces of turquoise the color of the sky so that this son would soar through the air as an eagle."

Grasping the eagle-shaped ornament, Walker spoke through his tears. "You knew my father."

Shell Listener's eyes focused on the pendant with the penetrating, timeless look that Walker had seen many times before in Great Owl's eyes. The muscles in his dark face strained with tenseness. The man's voice dropped. "Walker of Time, death is near . . . "

The squawking bird jumped up and down. It flapped its bright wings against Shell Listener's face, bringing his eyes back to the present.

72

Shell Listener peered up at Walker with fear. Trembling, he struggled off the rock bench. The bird's squawking turned into rasping scolding.

"Hush," Shell Listener hissed. He reached into the beaded pouch at his waist. "Walker, son of Lone Eagle," Shell Listener whispered, extending his hand to Walker. "Take these." He dropped two cool, hard objects into Walker's palm and squeezed the hand shut. "These come from where the great waters lick the white sands. They have the power to protect against the evil that seeks you and those near to you." His eyes darted toward White Badger and back to Walker. He leaned close. "The shell whispers of darkness—darkness broken by white bones. Strike these together as one. They shall light the darkness and protect you from evil."

Shell Listener let go of Walker's hand. His voice rose. "Go. Go before the evil that stalks you comes to me!"

Harsh squawking filled the hushed air as Walker moved away. He felt all eyes on him as he and White Badger left the amphitheater. How many others had heard Shell Listener's words?

Just outside the amphitheater, Walker opened his hand. Two smooth quartz stones rested in his palm. The stones were as smooth as silk and cylindrical with tapered ends. Turning the larger stone over in his hand, Walker saw it had a deep, longitudinal trough worn into it. He put them together. "The smaller one fits into the groove of the larger one," Walker said.

"I've never seen anything like them before." White Badger stared at the strange stones. "And I've never heard of a Shell Listener, but Father will know of both."

Walker smiled at his friend. Many others would have deserted him the instant Shell Listener spoke of death—many others still might. Superstition and fear of the unexplained seemed to rule these ancient people to a great degree, but White Badger always looked to the logical first.

"I wonder where he got his information." Walker slipped the stones into his leather waist pouch. Just as he accepted Great Owl's mystic powers, he could not ignore Shell Listener's warnings.

"Walker, White Badger," Son of Great Bear called loudly, coming from the game court just down the hill. Something about the way he carried himself was different—out of character. "High chief of my people, you are invited to the game court. The gaming pieces are falling for me today. Even Silent Thunder cannot win against me!" Son of Great Bear's voice matched his exaggerated bearing. "You must come. The men want to meet you."

Walker hesitated, a strange feeling of anxiety making him pause.

"It is rude to refuse them," Son of Great Bear insisted, hands on his hips.

Walking down the hill to the game court, Walker felt White Badger's uneasiness. They exchanged glances as Son of Great Bear bragged and strutted in a manner so unlike himself.

Women and children stood or sat on the top of the game court's six-foot-high, five-foot-wide walls watching the happenings below. Laughter, silence, cheers, and hisses alternated.

Son of Great Bear stopped just outside the entrance of the game court. "There is more, much more, to be had here than up there," he pointed to the amphitheater with his chin.

"It is a waste of time bartering when one can win so easily here." He entered the inverted U-shaped doorway.

"I've never seen Son of Great Bear like this," whispered White Badger, looking after his brother-in-law. He shook his head and entered the doorway.

Unlike the walls of Tall House and the amphitheater, these walls were primarily made of chunks of uneven sandstone mortared together. Walker could tell that less time and effort had been expended in building this unusual structure, but he knew that it too would stand for hundreds of years. Archaeologists in the future would question its usage. It was egg-shaped, thirty feet across in the middle and sixty or seventy feet long. Walker could see another entrance at the opposite end of the court. The bright sun and crisp air filled the roofless court, yet an overwhelming feeling swirled around Walker, wrapping its hostile tentacles around him.

"Welcome, young men." Silent Thunder stressed the word young as he advanced toward them. Walker had forgotten how strikingly handsome he was with his strong, classic face, elegant dress, and impressive jewelry. He fit perfectly into the artificial happiness and deceptive pleasure of the game court.

"I am surprised to see you both here. Flute Maiden," Silent Thunder's voice hinted close familiarity, "assured me that neither of you would come to the games. That you would be too occupied with more *important* things than to have fun in a game of chance." He faced White Badger. "You haven't answered any of my invitations to visit my village. We must discuss our mutual interest before you leave for Lomaki."

Walker sensed that White Badger was holding back his distaste as he answered, "You'd better come to Lomaki to discuss our mutual interest with my father."

A smile snaked across Silent Thunder's stately face. "Ah, yes. Some old ways never die—or do they?" He laughed, showing perfect white teeth. He swept his arms out as if to open the court to them. "Come and join our fun. I hope you brought plenty to wager."

The court was packed with men kneeling in tight circles. They made their way to where Son of Great Bear knelt. He didn't even notice them standing over him as he concentrated on the brightly decorated, tubular-shaped gaming discs that were being thrown to the ground and gathered up according to how they fell.

"I'll do better than that," Son of Great Bear vowed, picking up the pieces. His face turned sour, and he hammered the ground with his fist when the designs on the pieces fell against him.

The noise of the numerous bone-and-ceramic game pieces clattered, followed by the reaction of the spectators. Everywhere Walker looked, faces were carved in determination, momentary happiness, or intense dejection.

"At one time this court was used for games of physical skill, strength, and mental strategy." White Badger's voice was edged in disgust. "One was played with balls that were kicked and tossed. Many came to watch."

"Yes, and few were able to participate," Silent Thunder said over the sound of the falling game pieces. "Old ways are not the best. They are dying, making way for better ways. Ways that are more . . ."

"More profitable for a select few." The words burst out of Walker's mouth before they were totally formed in his mind.

Silent Thunder glared at him. "Only for those who are man enough and have the courage to take risks. It appears that the old, foolish ways are more suitable for the young and timid." His loud voice filled the now-quiet court.

All eyes were on Walker. Men clutching gaming pieces gaped at him. Women and children sitting on the walls glared down at him with defiance, confusion, and fear.

Tension swelled in the court. Walker knew that gambling in itself was not bad, but it brought out man's greed, his desire to have more with little effort. Gambling also attracted those who wanted power and control.

Sweat trickled down into Walker's face. How could he or anyone tell them? Could these people with their limited knowledge even comprehend that disregarding the old ways of seeking peace and harmony would disintegrate their cultures that had stood firm for hundreds of years? That in the fight for cultural survival, each person had to work for the good of the whole, not just for their own profit and gain? Walker stared at the mixture of faces around him and doubt washed over him. Was his knowledge of the future clouding and shading reality as it was *now*? Walker's body shook. Someone touched his shoulder. He whirled around, his fist clenched.

Startled, Scar Cheek jumped back. His face and chest were covered in dirty sweat. He fought to get his words out in-between raw pants. "Great Owl is dying!"

# 10

Walker knelt beside Great Owl on the roof of Lomaki, where he had asked to be taken to offer his morning prayer. Great Owl's sunken face was gray in the mixture of moon and predawn light. The air had a deadly sting to it.

Flute Maiden pulled a rabbit fur blanket up around Great Owl's shoulders, her own thin body trembling in the cold. She knew, as did the others, that nothing more could be done for her father. Her face was drawn in pain and grief. Swaying back and forth, Morning Flower cradled her baby daughter against her chest. Tears created a glittering path down her hollow cheeks. White Badger knelt next to his sisters at Great Owl's side. Grief shadowed his strong face as he held his father's hand.

Sitting on the opposite side of Great Owl, Walker's throat tightened as he watched his friends' sorrow. The wound of losing his own father bled as he felt Masau'u's deathly fingers reaching toward Great Owl. Walker closed his eyes. His weary mind whirled with the memories of the long hours since Scar Cheek had found them at the game court.

"After you left three days ago, Great Owl seemed happier and stronger than he has since we left our canyon," Scar Cheek had told Walker and White Badger as they searched for Flute Maiden at Tall House. "He walked a bit yesterday and spent time telling the children the old stories."

Scar Cheek's voice became lower. "Last night there were noises, but this time they were different, not human sounding. Even Dog's barking didn't stop them. This morning Great Owl couldn't lift his head from his sleeping mat. He kept calling for both of you and saying that evil was near."

White Badger, Flute Maiden, and Walker had left Tall House immediately. It had taken well into the night to reach Lomaki. Those tense, physically and emotionally draining hours as they raced against time and the rough terrain had a nightmarish quality in Walker's memory. But they were nothing to compare to the pain he now felt.

*Taawa, give me the strength to endure what must come,* Walker prayed silently. He felt a cold weight on his hand. Opening his eyes, he saw Great Owl's veined, weathered hand resting over his own.

"Masau'u is near. He does not seek *just* this old man." Great Owl's worried eyes penetrated Walker's. "My son," his voice was an ominous whisper. "Use your inner sight. Rid your heart of anger, hate, and jealousy so your eyes will see before Masau'u steals . . ." Great Owl's body shuddered. His eyes gazed, unfocused, as if he were seeing something in the future.

Walker gripped Great Owl's ice-cold hand. "Great Owl!"

Great Owl's eyes refocused and peered with determined

clarity at Walker. His voice was laced with death. "You must walk time. The paho in my basket will carry you."

Shock shot through Walker. Was Great Owl trying to prevent Walker's own death by sending him back through time? Walker's mind raced. Or did Tag need him? Had Great Owl seen Tag in serious trouble somewhere in time? When was he to walk time—now, tomorrow, next week? He couldn't leave before he got his people to the mesas. They needed him —or did they?

Walker felt his body tremble as his mind pursued a new line of thought. Was Great Owl releasing him from leadership because he couldn't—no, *hadn't*— used his inner sight? Had he failed so completely that Great Owl was banishing him back to the future where he really belonged? These and a hundred other questions flashed through Walker's mind as Great Owl's spirit slipped into Masau'u's waiting fingers.

\* \* \*

Walker's heart warmed as he stood on the roof and looked down at the hundred or more people gathered around Lomaki's entrance. They were Great Owl's friends, his extended family of those living in the old ways of seeking peace and harmony.

Word of Great Owl's death had been sent to Strong House with the first light of day, and the news quickly spread to the other villages. Leaning Tree and Morning Talk arrived first, before the sun reached its midmorning zenith.

"We have come to bid our honored friend farewell," Leaning Tree said in a humble voice.

Walker was amazed that so many had come so far, so fast, to pay their respects to Great Owl. Now they waited patiently for the seer to be returned to Mother Earth.

"Things are ready." White Badger's voice was strained but controlled as he moved up next to Walker on the roof. "Son of Great Bear and the others are finally back from Tall House."

Son of Great Bear's strange behavior at the game court nagged at Walker. He pushed it into the back of his mind. This was no time to worry about it. "Good. The sun will be setting soon." Walker turned to White Badger. Grief dug deep lines into White Badger's proud face. Walker's heart twisted. He put his arms around his friend. "Losing a father is never easy. I wish I could carry all your sorrow with mine." Walker felt White Badger's body heavy with sobs. He held his friend for two, three, four minutes until White Badger's sobs subsided.

"He loved you as a son, as you loved him like a father," White Badger said, squaring his broad shoulders. "We will carry the sorrow together."

\* \* \*

The thousands of tiny, brilliant beads on Great Owl's ceremonial cap glittered in the late-day sun. His body lay in a narrow crevice in a huge lava rock formation on the cinder hill over looking Lomaki. His old knees, which had bent so often in prayer, were now covered with his long, red ceremonial kilt. White moccasins, decorated with hundreds of beads, covered his feet. His intricately carved staff lay across his still chest.

Walker watched Flute Maiden lean down and tenderly cover the peaceful face of her father with a green cloth. He couldn't make out the words she spoke, but he felt the sorrow in her voice. From within her mantel she withdrew a thumb-sized crystal and laid it on her father's stilled heart as a token of her love and respect. Her tear-clouded eyes met Walker's as she rose. The ache in Walker's throat tightened, and no air seemed to get to his lungs.

White Badger, following Flute Maiden, knelt beside the narrow grave. He placed a polished stone effigy of an eagle next to the crystal. His body shook as he rose to let Morning Flower, Son of Great Bear, and Small Cub take his place beside the grave.

Small Cub cried and dropped something into the grave. He scrambled to his feet and buried his face into Flute Maiden's skirt. She stroked his hair and whispered something into his ear. He pulled away sobbing and ran down the steep hill toward Lomaki. Son of Great Bear followed.

One by one, Walker's people approached the rock grave, bidding Great Owl farewell and leaving tokens of their love and esteem. Arrow Maker struggled to kneel down beside the grave. His humped back shook with sobs as he lowered a bow with arrows bound to it into the grave. Fawn gave a finely shaped, white bowl. Littlest Star left a small, tightly woven basket, and Rising Sun gave an antelope horn carved with delicate designs. Walker was overwhelmed by his people's love for Great Owl. After kneeling at the grave, each person made his way down the steep hill to Lomaki.

Morning Talk was the first of the visiting people to make her offering. She wiped her eyes with the corner of her mantel and placed a small, painted basket within the burying place. Rising, she put her arms around Flute Maiden and held her in a tight embrace. Walker wished he had the courage to do the same.

It seemed like it had taken forever for the long line of people to kneel beside the grave. Now with the sun lying on the horizon, only White Badger, Morning Flower, Flute Maiden, and Walker remained. Walker knelt, staring down into the grave. Great Owl's body was covered with gifts—polished arrowheads, wooden containers of mineral pigment, shell tinklers and jewelry, small baskets, pots, jars, and vases. Walker's offering seemed so insignificant compared to the others. He looked down at the bone whistle he had made for Great Owl weeks ago but had never found the opportunity to give him. It was a simple thing but had a sweet, pure tone that Great Owl would appreciate. Walker placed the whistle in the grave. Had Great Owl known how much he had loved him?

Flute Maiden and Morning Flower, arm in arm, turned to leave. As Flute Maiden passed with tears streaking down her face, Walker reached out and touched her shoulder. She paused, but didn't raise her eyes from the ground. Holding her shoulder rigid, she moved on.

Walker took a deep breath as he watched Flute Maiden and Morning Flower walk down the hill to Lomaki. He turned to White Badger. "Let me help you."

"No, I need to do it alone." White Badger lifted the first large stone that had been gathered earlier to entomb the grave. "I will stay here for a while after I . . ." White Badger's words died in the cold air.

A chill raced up Walker's back. A deep, desperate feeling within pleaded not to leave White Badger on this hill of death. But the determined look in White Badger's eyes ordered Walker to leave.

\* \* \*

The now familiar, eerie tinkling sound reached Walker's ears as his mind hovered just above sleep. He jerked up. Dog was poised at the edge of the roof, growling.

Walker felt Dog's trembling tenseness as he put his arm around her. The tinkling came from the cinder hill to the east where Great Owl's grave was. The hair on Dog's neck bristled upward like porcupine quills as she began barking fiercely.

"What's wrong?" Scar Cheek startled Walker. Loud, inhuman moans answered the question.

"Help me lower the ladder," Walker whispered.

"Where is White Badger?"

The ladder hit the ground. "He hasn't come back from Great Owl's grave." Fear and anxiety pumped through Walker. He gathered up Dog and started down the ladder. "Get the other men!"

Dog jumped from Walker's arm the minute his foot touched the ground. She raced toward the cinder hill to the east.

Walker could hear Dog's angry barking halfway up the cinder hill as he began working his own way up. The thin layers of cinders slipped under his moccasins. His heart hammered against his ribs, and a tingling tightness spread across his shoulders and up his neck.

As Walker came within sight of the large rock formation, silence filled the moonlit night. Sniffing the ground, Dog circled the wide base of the rock formation where Great Owl's body lay. She lifted her head when Walker approached, then continued her search for scents that should have been there but weren't.

The stark moonlight gave everything an eerie, one-dimensional, shadowy look. Coldness seeped into Walker's bones.

Nothing moved, except for Dog running this way and that with her nose to the ground.

"White Badger!" Walker's call echoed back to him from the surrounding buttes.

A neat mound of rocks covered Great Owl's narrow grave. Each rock cast a ghostly shadow downward. "White Badger," Walker called again, climbing up beside the grave.

A glint in the moonlight caught Walker's eye. He knelt. Wedged in between the rocks of the grave was White Badger's stone knife. Walker picked it up. It was cold.

Silent Thunder's warning echoed in Walker's mind. *Physical strength is like a dry blade of grass when pitted against evil spirits.*

# 11

The sun stood directly overhead as Walker and Scar Cheek came into view of Lomaki. At the sight of the classic, pueblo-style village, dread seeped into Walker's bones. He sensed the same feeling in Scar Cheek. Their hunt for food had been successful, but their other, more important, search had failed.

Walker saw the small, familiar figure standing on the roof. He waved and scurried down the ladder to the ground. "Did you find Uncle White Badger?" Small Cub called. His clam shell pendant bounced on his chest as he bounded over the rocks and cacti in his path. Dog followed on his heels. They met Walker about thirty yards from Lomaki.

Walker bent down and hugged the boy. "No."

Tears welled up in Small Cub's enormous eyes. "Father and the others didn't, either. The others are saying that evil spirits stole White Badger away, and that the spirits will come back for each of us, too."

Walker squeezed Small Cub's thin shoulder. "I don't believe that."

"But father said . . . "

"Small Cub," Flute Maiden's voice was stern but not unkind. "It's not polite to repeat things that you hear your elders speak to one another."

Walker looked up to where she stood, a few feet away. Their eyes met. The wall of silence and misunderstanding stood between them.

Small Cub dug around in his waist pouch, "I will go with you to hunt for White Badger, and I'll use the shiny wayfinder Tag left me." He held up the Boy Scout compass. "I know that I can find White Badger with this."

"We'll see. Now please take these rabbits to your mother."

"When we go, I will bring my hunting stick, too." Small Cub took the two dead rabbits from Walker. "I'll get bigger ones than these scrawny things."

"Small Cub." Flute Maiden nodded to Lomaki.

"I will go with you, Small Cub." Scar Cheek took his hand. "I hear that you are getting very skillful with a hunting stick." Small Cub's answer was a blur of words as the two walked toward Lomaki.

"It has been two days since White Badger . . ." Flute Maiden looked at the rock formation on the hill above them. The wind whipped her short skirt around her bare legs.

Walker noticed that she wasn't wearing any of Silent Thunder's jewelry as she had been. What did it mean? Walker wondered. Was it out of mourning?

"Small Cub is right about what is being said. The others know that White Badger wouldn't just leave." Flute Maiden faced Walker. "There are many whispers of evil spirits—witches."

"I know." Walker's words sounded shallow. The people had done well living at Lomaki, despite the stories of it being haunted, but White Badger's mysterious disappearance was more than they could handle.

"I'm so frightened, Walker," Tears slipped down Flute Maiden's cheeks.

Walker hesitated, then drew her to him. "So am I." He leaned his face against the top of her head. "But not of evil spirits." Walker held her tight, closing his eyes. He felt a sense of peace that he had not felt for months. "Flute Maiden, I . . ."

The sound of cinders crunching brought Walker's head up. He saw a group of men striding down the hill toward Lomaki. The leader was easy to recognize by his powerful shoulders, turquoise-adorned chest, and confident stride.

Walker felt Flute Maiden stiffen in his arms.

"Walker, please don't . . ."

He released her.

"Set the kill here." Silent Thunder's order choked the space between Walker and Flute Maiden.

Son of Great Bear appeared out of Lomaki. "Welcome, Silent Thunder." He bowed low as he blew on the man's hand.

"We did not hear the sad news till last sunset. I hope that your people will accept this meat with our sympathy." Silent Thunder's voice sounded practiced in giving condolence.

"Your gift is accepted in the spirit it was given in," Walker said, moving up behind the man. It was a struggle to keep his voice steady with anger streaking through every cell of his body.

Silent Thunder whirled around, his hand on the long obsidian knife in his wide belt. His face was a smooth mask of sorrow but his eyes were pinpoints of hatred. "We won't bother your people in their troubles. Step aside. I wish to speak to Flute Maiden."

Walker clenched his hands and moved. Silent Thunder pushed past him, and the hair on Walker's neck stood on end. He fought to keep from turning to watch. Scar Cheek appeared at his side.

"Evil travels with that man," Scar Cheek whispered. The red scar across his face looked angrier than usual. "Let's move the antelope."

Walker was again thankful for Scar Cheek's awareness and sensitivity. He reached down for the front legs of the dead animal. Its eyes stared vacantly back at him. The smell of death burned Walker's nose. White Badger's face burst into Walker's mind. His dark eyes stared at Walker with the same vacant look as the antelope.

"Someone else is coming," Scar Cheek's anxious voice shattered the graphic aberration in Walker's mind.

Leaning Tree led. Two men, a few feet behind, were dragging a pole sled behind them.

Even before Walker reached Leaning Tree, he knew what lay on the sled, but his heart and mind fought against the reality of it.

"Wait, Walker!" Leaning Tree reached out to stop him, but Walker rushed past him.

White Badger's head lay at a strange angle to his body. His chest and legs were covered with dry blood and dirt.

Walker knew that White Badger's eyes, though closed, stared vacantly in death.

"No!" Walker's cry echoed off the cinder hills and back to Lomaki.

"One of our men found him at the foot of a steep, rocky butte near our village," Leaning Tree said, as Walker knelt beside his friend's broken body. The words floated in the cold breeze but didn't connect in Walker's mind.

Leaning Tree knelt beside Walker. "He must have fallen."

Walker heard the words but didn't bond with them.

"This kind of thing happened to many of the men here at Lomaki before you came," Leaning Tree whispered.

Morning Flower's cry brought Walker's mind into focus. She stood above him, her face in her hands with Son of Great Bear by her side. Son of Great Bear's face was ashen as he stared down at his brother-in-law's body.

*Flute Maiden!* Walker pushed through the knot of people gathering around him. *She'll need . . .*

Flute Maiden was cradled in Silent Thunder's arms, her face buried in his chest. Her body was wracked with sobs.

Silent Thunder's deep voice rose above the shocked confusion. "You did not listen to my warning. By bringing your people to this evil place, White Badger's death, and all those that are sure to follow, is on your hands, Walker. The spirits that haunt Lomaki are not afraid of a boy who walks through time."

# 12

Walker laid the last large, volcanic rock on White Badger's grave. He sat back on his heels and looked toward the west. The sky was on fire. The luminous sunset washed the gravestones in an eerie reddish light. Walker peered down at his hands, and they, too, seemed to be bathed in blood.

Was the blood of his people truly on his hands? Walker's exhausted and tormented mind questioned as he stared at White Badger's and Great Owl's graves lying almost side by side. He knew they were the graves he had seen time after time in his limited sight. But he had ignored the warnings, the uncontrollable and painful predictions, and had done nothing to prevent his friends' deaths.

Would they still be alive if he had not convinced them to leave Walnut Canyon? Goosebumps pricked Walker's body. Had he been wrong in assuming leadership of the people instead of letting Gray Wolf, who was older and more mature, fill the role? For all he knew, Gray Wolf and the others had survived the plague and were still living within the safety of the cliffs of Walnut Canyon. Why had he been so eager to take on the responsibility and so anxious to leave the canyon?

Doubt and confusion surged through Walker. Had Great Owl left him the new paho so that he could walk back into the future *now*, leaving the leadership to Son of Great Bear or someone else more capable? Had Great Owl looked into the days and months ahead and seen that the only way for any of the people to survive was to send Walker back where he belonged?

The sun sank out of sight, leaving Walker in its dying light. The memories of the distant future swirled around him. Each thought, feeling, and image spoke of how easy and comfortable life had been with his Uncle Náat on Second Mesa. What the bahanas considered primitive in the 1900s was pure luxury compared to life now, which was a constant battle for mere existence.

"Náat, why did you send me back here? What good am I doing here?" Walker cried, lifting his face to the darkened sky. "Did you send me back just to learn the anguish and pain of losing to Masau'u? The god of death first stole my father, whom I had just found after so many years. Next Great Owl slipped into Masau'u fingers in fear. Now White Badger! Why?" Walker clenched his fist at the star-studded heavens. "White Badger was too young, too good. Did he die just so I could practice the art of sealing graves? Why Náat? Why did you send me here?"

Walker's body crumpled into a heap as he buried his face into his hands and wept.

\* \* \*

"The journey to the Mesas will be long and hard. Many may not have the strength to survive," Son of Great Bear stated the next afternoon. The men sat in a tight circle on Lomaki's roof. The decision of whether to leave Lomaki was being debated. "Walker can't promise that the Hopi will let us stay with them during the winter or that we will be able to build our own village there when spring comes. Where will we go if they don't let us stay?" Son of Great Bear seemed like his old confident self again, yet Walker could not sense the inner peace or harmony that had so distinctively marked him in the past. What had happened to Son of Great Bear at Tall House that had destroyed that inner peace? wondered Walker, listening to him.

Son of Great Bear looked from one man to another. His large, intelligent eyes were intense. "This *house* has brought death to our people, as it did to those before us. It is not the land that frowns on us. We have learned new and better ways of doing things from the different villages, and there is much more we must learn." He paused, shifting his weight. "Life can be very good in this area." His eyes avoided Walker. "We have proven our worth to others. There is a village here that will welcome us while the snows lay on the ground."

A bad taste seeped into Walker's mouth. He knew *which* village Son of Great Bear was talking about, but the *why* was not clear. Walker was astonished that Son of Great Bear would even consider such a thing. Until the trading trip to Tall House, Son of Great Bear had the same aversion and distrust toward Silent Thunder that Great Owl and White Badger had shown. How had Silent Thunder gained control over Son of Great Bear?

Walker took a deep breath and shut his eyes. It didn't matter *how*. He was too exhausted physically and mentally to wonder or argue. Perhaps Son of Great Bear was right. There was no guarantee that life at Hopi would be any better than right here. Walker's thoughts shifted to the new paho that looked exactly like the prayer stick that had mysteriously zapped him back in time. The two sticks carved in the images of a male and a female were painted blue-green and bound together with a long leather thong. White eagle feathers tied at the base of the two faces completed the simple but powerful paho. Walker visualized the prayer stick now lying in his own carrying basket along with his few other belongings. It would take him only a few days to hike back to Walnut Canyon and to the cave. He could even possibly make it back to Hopi before school started. The track-and-wrestling coach would be glad to see him at least.

"Small Cub is gone!" Morning Flower's cry brought Walker back to reality. Morning Flower, followed by Arrow Maker's wife, Early Snow, rushed up the ladder to the roof. She ran to Son of Great Bear, gripping him by the arm. "Small Cub has been taken by evil spirits!"

"He was with our son, Fast Lizard, and Dog," Early Snow exclaimed. "They left early to go rabbit hunting. Fast Lizard thought it would help Small Cub forget about White . . . " She stopped with a sob.

"Fast Lizard?" Arrow Maker put his arm around his wife. His misshapen body was trembling as badly as hers.

"He's below. Flute Maiden is caring for him. He has a wound on his head, but the spirits . . . "

"Tell me what happened to Small Cub!" Son of Great Bear cried, shaking Morning Flower.

Morning Flower's round face was white. Her dark eyes were pools of terror.

Early Snow answered the demand. "They were hunting beyond Strong House. Fast Lizard said that Dog started to growl and they heard strange sounds."

"It was a roaring sound like thunder, yet like moans," Fast Lizard said, coming up the ladder. He was a tall, responsible thirteen-year-old with his mother's large, expressive eyes and small mouth. The back of his hair was matted with blood. Flute Maiden followed him up the ladder. "We were in a narrow area with a wall of rocks surrounding us. The sound came first from the rocks to the east. Then it answered itself to the west. It wasn't a human sound." Fast Lizard swayed on his feet.

Flute Maiden put her arms around him. "Sit down." Her frightened eyes met Walker's.

Walker knelt beside the boy. He kept his voice controlled and calm, despite the turmoil raging within him. "Tell us what happened next." The others crowded around.

"Small Cub was ahead of me, picking up a rabbit that we had chased into the rocky enclosure and killed. I called to him to leave the rabbit—that we had to get out of there. Dog started barking. She wouldn't leave Small Cub's side." Fast Lizard's sturdy body shook. "The roaring was coming from everywhere, like evil spirits flying in circles all around us."

Fast Lizard looked at Walker, then at Son of Great Bear. "Small Cub was like ice. He couldn't move. I started to run to get him, but then," Fast Lizard shook his head, touching the back of it. "I woke up with cinders cutting into my chest and the back of my head throbbing." His next words came in a hoarse whisper. "Small Cub and Dog had disappeared!"

It took Walker, Son of Great Bear, and Scar Cheek less than an hour to reach the unusual formation where Small Cub disappeared.

A distinctive, steep, ten-foot-high cropping of lava rock enclosed a flat, oval-shaped strip of cinders. A very narrow, rocky opening broke through the lava wall. Chills ran up Walker's back as he looked at the craggy rock wall rising above his head. There were hundreds of places for someone to hide.

*Taawa, protect Small Cub. Help us find him,* Walker prayed, lowering his head to his chest. His eyes caught a brownish-red splotch among the black cinders. He knelt. The blood was dried but not old.

Son of Great Bear knelt beside Walker. "Small Cub's?"

Walker felt Son of Great Bear's anguish. "The rabbit's. See, here is a small foot mark. The way it is angled and dug in, it looks like Small Cub squatted down to pick up the rabbit." With care not to disturb any other prints, Walker searched the nearby ground but found nothing. It was as if the sharp cinders had been swept clean.

Scar Cheek called from near the entrance of the rocky enclosure. "Here is where Fast Lizard must have fallen, and there are his foot marks leading out."

A single set of prints leaving the entrance mingled with their own tracks coming in. "Yes, they must be Fast Lizard's, the ones he made when he left to get help," Walker said. "There should be more."

"Evil Spirits leave no ground marks," Son of Great Bear whispered, his eyes darting around him.

"Two boys chasing a rabbit do. We should be able to find their tracks leading in."

"Evil spirits have no need for rabbit meat or a dog," Scar Cheek added, gripping his spear tighter. "Let's look outside."

Only one windblown set of prints led from the strange

formation in the direction of Lomaki. "I wonder how long Fast Lizard was unconscious?" Walker studied the vast prairie surrounding them. His mind pieced their findings together. Following the boys and hiding in the rocks would have been simple, but what had the kidnappers used to make the thundering-moaning sounds? Some kind of noisemaker? With so many different villages and clans in the area, each with its own unique social and religious practices, anything was possible. Walker wished that Tag were here. This was just the type of weird sound that he would have an answer for —if there was an archaeological explanation for it. Walker's scalp tightened. *If there were a human explanation.*

"Let's split up and see what we can find," suggested Scar Cheek.

* * *

The sun stood far to the west, and Walker realized that hours had passed in his meticulous but futile searching. He needed to start back to meet Son of Great Bear and Scar Cheek as they had agreed upon before splitting up. Maybe they had had better luck. He hadn't found tracks of any kind. Strange, he thought. Usually one could find some kind of animal, lizard, snake, or even bird tracks. A cold wind swept over Walker. Maybe Yaponcha the wind god had been playing games with him, blowing away all the evidence. The part of Walker that believed and followed the old ways could accept this, but the other part of him, the bahana educated side, resisted.

Again, as so many times before, Walker felt as if he were balancing between two worlds. One world was controlled by logic and scientific evidence, while the other was filled with long-held traditions and beliefs that explained everything from how the sun got into the sky to why ants have skinny waists. Standing alone with the cold wind beating against his cheek, Walker realized he would always play a game of tug-of-war between the here and now and the world of tomorrow.

*You will walk time again*, Great Owl's last words murmured through the wind.

"Not until I find Small Cub," Walker cried out. "Not until then!"

He scanned the hilly horizon. Nothing. His blood felt cold, his bones frozen. How could anyone find a boy so small in such a vast wilderness? It was impossible without—without inner sight. Walker trembled. *Inner sight.* Turmoil and doubt echoed through Walker's heart as he tried to force his eyes to see—see anything.

A slinking movement to the left caught Walker's eye. Walker swung around clutching his spear.

A brown animal moved out from behind two rocks. He whistled and started running toward Dog, who cowered and whined.

"It's all right, girl." Dog looked up with sorrowful eyes. Walker knelt and stroked her head. Blood covered his hand. "What happened?" He gently felt the bloody spot. A large chunk of skin had been nicked off. Walker cupped his hand and poured water into it from his canteen. Dog lapped up the water. "Spirits don't need rocks to scare dogs away. It took a lot to chase you off, didn't it?"

Dog thumped her tail but had a worried looked in her sorrowful black eyes. She licked Walker's hand even after the last drop of water was gone.

Sitting back on his haunches, Walker thought through the situation. He was sure that Dog had followed whoever had taken Small Cub. It would be easy to follow Dog's trail, but if he went back to get the other two men it would be too late. Even with the full moon tonight, it would be impossible to follow dog's tracks once the sun set. Time was working against him and against Small Cub. Was he a fool to go alone?

"Great Taawa, guide my steps," Walker prayed, "and my eyes."

*Go before it is too late, my son,* a cold wind whispered over the prairie.

Walker trembled. Was it Náat's or Lone Eagle's voice he had heard?

Dog's trail was easy to follow, though it zigzagged behind rocks and bushes. Clearly she had followed at a distance, keeping out of sight of the kidnappers. Walker was amazed at the animal's intelligence, or was it just survival instinct? A deep suspicion murmured that Dog knew and feared whoever had taken Small Cub.

At once Dog realized that Walker was following her trail. She ran ahead, leading the way in a straight and well-known route to where Small Cub was being held.

The air was cold and daylight was turning gray as Walker came within sight of the three-story pueblo village. It was built on a huge cinder butte that stood within the high, protective walls of a box canyon. The red sandstone village stood out from the black, rugged walls of the canyon like a bleeding wound.

Walker had never seen the village before, but he knew without a doubt who ruled as high chief. The smell of death burned Walker's nose.

# 13

Walker tried to slow his thundering heart. Even though the atmosphere was wintry, he knew that the coldness growing in his core wasn't caused by the setting sun.

There was no movement around Silent Thunder's secluded village. It was smaller than Strong House but looked even more invincible with its high, thick walls that had no windows on the ground level and just a few small openings in the upper stories. The only low, T-shaped entrance was barricaded with what looked like a heavy wooden plank. If the village had a plaza it was sequestered within the protection of the walls. There didn't seem to be anyone standing guard on the roof, but Walker instinctively pulled himself further behind the boulder he crouched beside.

The village was much larger than Lomaki. Walker guessed that it could house fifty or more people. At this time of day, people would be settling in for the long night ahead, but it was odd that there was no activity around the village.

Instead of the air being filled with the sounds of children playing, mothers calling, and people milling around, the air reeked of silent hostility.

Dog growled.

Walker pulled her close. "I know. It wasn't a pleasant place for you." The muscles in Dog's back were tense. "I doubt it's a good place for anyone or anything." He knew that somewhere within the thick walls that seem to cry out with sorrow and anguish, Small Cub was being held—if he was still alive.

"I can walk right into the village and demand Small Cub back," Walker whispered to Dog. She looked up and whined. "Or I can sneak in, find Small Cub, and get out." Walker studied the village. "It would be easy if I were Superman or Indiana Jones." The feeling of certain defeat ate away at Walker's determination as time hammered down on his shoulders. Whatever he decided to do, it needed to be done now.

Walker clutched his eagle pendant. His father's dying words, *Walk strong . . . Always walk with Taawa,* echoed through his mind.

He rose from his hiding place. Dog followed. "No, stay here."

The massive walls surrounding the roofless plaza closed in on Walker. The feeling of oppression seeped from every skin-draped doorway opening into the plaza. The ladders leading to the upper story looked like long leg bones lashed together. The courtyard was empty except for Walker and the two well-armed men who had seized him even before he reached the village entrance. They now stood uncomfortably close on either side of him. Slow Bear was a huge man. His brown eyes, set far apart, showed little intelligence. The other man, Black Spider, was small in height, but his ample girth spoke of plenty of food. His beady eyes kept darting toward Walker.

"I didn't expect you so soon." Silent Thunder stalked toward Walker. A tall, thin, pock-faced man followed close behind with the same confident smirk that was on Silent Thunder's handsome face.

"I've come for Small Cub." Walker's eyes locked with Silent Thunder's.

Silent Thunder's laughter echoed off the walls of the houses. His hand rested on the knife at his waist. "Did you really think it would be that easy? Black Spider, Tangled Grass, go see if anyone is waiting for him outside. Search everywhere. If there is, kill them. We'll finish it all in one night."

The hair on Walker's neck stood on end. What did Silent Thunder mean, *finish it all in one night*?

Silent Thunder grinned. "You've made things much easier than I had planned. Slow Bear, put him down into the kiva and guard him."

One of the rungs of the pole ladder going down into the kiva was missing. Walker's foot slipped. He plummeted into darkness and landed with a jarring thud. The unexpected smell of decay filled Walker's nose.

The ladder was dragged up out of the kiva. Slow Bear's homely face glared down through the entrance. "I will be right up here, so don't try to fly out."

The evening light coming through the square hatch barely put a dint in the cold darkness. Something furry scurried over Walker's moccasin. He jumped, almost tripping on something behind his feet. A rumbling sound vibrated through the kiva.

Walker turned and saw a dark ball, the size of two fists together, gyrating on the stone floor. *A thunder ball,* Walker realized. He had seen similar stone balls in other villages. The roaring sound they made as they rolled across the kiva's stone floors was intended to sound like thunder and to beckon rain clouds. The ball's rotation and thunder sound stopped as it careened into a huge mound of rotting corncobs and squash rinds. Repulsion washed over Walker. The sacred meeting room had become a dumping ground. Broken pottery, rotting food, torn mats, worn baskets, and other unrecognizable trash was strewn in piles throughout the kiva. Walker felt nauseated. What kind of leader would allow the ceremonial room, the most holy place in the village, to be filled with garbage? If Silent Thunder had no regard for the kiva, then he had no respect for any traditional beliefs or even life itself.

A scratching-scraping noise came from the opposite side of the kiva. It started from the top of the kiva wall and slithered downward. Walker's scalp tightened.

The noise stopped, replaced with the sound of rock grating on rock. Walker picked his way through the garbage across the key-shaped kiva toward the sound. The noise came from the square air vent at the base of the wall. The vent was a narrow shaft that opened to the plaza floor above, allowing outside air to ventilate the kiva's fire pit. A rock slab on one side of the vent moved forward. Walker jolted back, almost tripping on garbage.

Another slab moved forward and was pushed out by a dirty hand. Walker knelt and jerked out three more loose rocks. Two skinny arms pulled thin shoulders through the enlarged air vent. No Name looked up at Walker. His face was covered in old grime and new dirt from climbing down the shaft. "Where is my dog? Small Cub said you would know."

Walker pulled the boy out of the narrow opening. "Where's Small Cub?"

"Where is Dog?" No Name demanded, standing nose to nose with Walker, who was still kneeling.

"Waiting outside the village. Small Cub?"

"Silent Thunder put him in an empty room on the second story." No Name's voice became even lower. He huddled against the wall, pulling Walker down, too. "Silent Thunder will kill you both and the others, like he did the people that lived in Lomaki before you." He held his hand out to Walker. "Take this knife. I made it. It's not very big, but it's sharp."

Walker slipped the crude knife into the waistband of his legging. "Why did Silent Thunder kill the people at Lomaki?"

"The leaders of Lomaki saw him as he is—evil. They refused to trade with him and talked against him to the leaders of the other villages. They didn't want them to trade with him, either."

*Of course!* The pieces fell together in Walker's racing mind. Silent Thunder had made himself the kingpin of the trade business in the Wupatki area. With the desperate times, he used this economic lever to gain power of the villages. No wonder Leaning Tree and the others were afraid of him. Silent Thunder held the key to life—trade. He probably controlled the gambling, too. *A regular Mafia chief!*

Loud snoring filtered down through the kiva's entrance. "Slow Bear sleeps like a bear. A bee sting on his nose won't wake him," No Name said, straightening his crouched position.

"Where did Silent Thunder come from?"

"No one knows. He and his men came to our village when I was small. There are whispers that he came from the giant villages to the east. Our leaders welcomed him as they did all visitors. Mother said that Silent Thunder brought hate in his heart and death in his hands." No Name's lean body stiffened. "He killed my father and all the others that opposed his ways until all that was left were women, children, and a few men who became loyal to him."

Despite the loud snoring from above, Walker knew time was short. The kiva was getting darker by the minute as the daylight above died. "How many men does he have?"

"As many as all of your fingers, but Silent Thunder sent this many," he held up six fingers, "to Lomaki before you came."

*To finish it all*, Walker thought, fear piercing his reasoning. That left Silent Thunder and four others here. Black Spider and Tangled Grass were searching outside the village. How long would it take them to discover that Walker was alone? Slow Bear was asleep overhead. Who was the unseen fourth man? A chill ran up Walker's spine.

"Will the women help me against Silent Thunder and his men?"

"They are too frightened. They have learned to do only what they are told or be beaten and put down here to starve. I dug away the shaft so I could bring food and water to my mother and the others." Deep anger penetrated No Name's voice. "When the snow covered the ground last, Silent Thunder beat my mother and threw her down here. Before I could get here, her spirit left." His faced twisted in anger. "I'm not afraid to help you."

105

Walker touched the boy's wiry shoulder. "I know you aren't. Can you get to Small Cub?"

"I know where he is. It is another place that Silent Thunder puts people in to punish them." No Name squared his shoulders. "I can get into it without being seen. I've done it many times."

"Good. Take Small Cub to Strong House; it is closer than Lomaki. Leaning Tree will help you. The only chance for your people is if all the villages band together against Silent Thunder."

No Name shook his head. "Silent Thunder owns people in every village, but no one knows who. Death comes to anyone who even speaks ill of Silent Thunder. No one dares oppose him."

Mafia-style executions, Walker speculated. Even Tag wouldn't have believed it all. It was all too futuristic. *I should have figured it all out before—I should have seen it!*

"Slow Bear, you stupid fool, wake up!" Silent Thunder's voice roared down from above. "Get him up here. Now!"

"Hurry," Walker whispered, pushing No Name toward the vent. "Go to Lomaki. Tell Scar Cheek what you have told me. Tell him to . . ."

The ladder slid down through the kiva's opening. No Name squirmed backwards into the vent. With only his head sticking out, he whispered, "What are you going to do?"

The ladder hit the ground. No Name disappeared. Walker moved to the foot of the ladder. He could see the moon's full face in the sky above the hatch.

"Boy who walks time, come up here," Slow Bear's words slurred with sleepiness.

How much time did No Name need? Five minutes—ten?

Silent Thunder's voice growled. "Go get him!"

"But there are rats down there," whined Slow Bear.

"Go before I . . ."

The old ladder began creaking under Slow Bear's heavy weight. Walker made his way through the litter to the wall behind the ladder, picking up the thunder ball as he went.

"Where are you, boy?" Slow Bear asked through the almost total darkness now.

Walker heard him move away from the ladder toward the opposite wall. He tried not to breathe. Since Walker could see only a foot in front of himself he knew Slow Bear couldn't see him from across the fifteen-foot kiva. He heard Slow Bear's feet shuffling through the garbage on the floor. Using the wall as a guide, Walker moved along it in the opposite direction.

*Just like playing blind man's bluff.* The thought shot through Walker's mind. He caught himself from laughing out loud. The seconds turned into minutes as Walker inched along the wall like the little hand on a clock. Using the noise of Slow Bear's big feet, Walker kept directly across from him.

"Where are you?" The angry words echoed against the kiva's plastered walls.

Thud!

Cussing filled the air. Walker heard Slow Bear picking himself up. There was a high squeak, followed by Slow Bear's terrified screams. "Rat! Rats!"

A bright, flickering light burst into the kiva from above. Walker put his hand up to block out the sudden brightness. He was next to the wall directly in front of the ladder. Slow Bear crouched, like a frightened child, against the opposite wall.

Seeing Walker, Slow Bear lunged forward. His feet got tangled up in an old mat. He fell like a tree, face first into a heap of rotting corncobs and squash rinds.

"Enough games!" Silent Thunder's roar from above shook the kiva.

Slow Bear scrambled to his feet.

Heaving the thunder ball to Slow Bear, Walker called, "Catch!"

The huge man lunged forward to catch the ball, but slipped on slick squash rinds and landed with a thump on his massive rump.

*Taawa be with me now*, Walker prayed, as he scrambled up the ladder before Slow Bear got to his feet again.

The smoky torch that Silent Thunder held, cast flickering shadows around the empty plaza. Walker thought he saw movement in the dancing shadows along the far wall behind Silent Thunder. Was it No Name and Small Cub?

"I told you he'd come," a voice, with a familiar snarl to it, exclaimed from behind Walker.

Walker jerked around. In the swaying light, Gray Wolf's face looked even sharper and more angular than Walker remembered. Walker's memory of Gray Wolf trying to kill him at Walnut Canyon was crystal clear, though. Gray Wolf's small, hate-filled eyes gleamed with that same desire.

"You were wrong about one thing, Gray Wolf," Silent Thunder sounded amused. "The boy came alone, but we'll get Son of Great Bear soon enough, even though he's mine already."

Gray Wolf strutted past Walker and stood at Silent Thunder's side. They looked like two hideous bookends, thought Walker.

"Scar Cheek, too. I am sure his loyalties haven't changed." Gray Wolf toyed with the knife at his waist. "After that the rest of *my* people will gladly make me high chief."

Walker fought to keep his clenched fists at his side. "Do you really think that Silent Thunder will share even a handful of people with you?" He chuckled and stared into Gray Wolf's hard eyes. "If you believe that, you are stupider than I thought."

Gray Wolf's fist smashed into Walker's face. Walker tasted blood even before he hit the hard-packed ground.

"Let me kill him now!" Gray Wolf stood over Walker.

"Maybe I should let you kill each other and save me the trouble of killing both of you."

Gray Wolf whipped around and lunged at Silent Thunder.

Silent Thunder thrust the torch toward Gray Wolf's heaving chest. "Get back." He whirled the flames closer to Gray Wolf, forcing him back next to Walker, who was still on the ground. "The boy is smarter than you. Why would I share anything with you? The information you had was the only thing that has kept you alive this long." He gestured to Slow Bear, who was just climbing out of the kiva's hatch. "Take his knife."

Slow Bear lumbered toward Gray Wolf.

*Now*, the stars sang to Walker. *Now!*

# 14

Walker lunged with a roll toward Slow Bear. Hitting the huge man's knees was like smashing into a stone wall. Slow Bear swayed, then teetered, with one foot off the ground. Rising up on his haunches, Walker swung his elbow into Slow Bear's flabby stomach and shoved. The man toppled sideways down through the kiva's entrance, the bottom of his flat, dirty feet disappearing last into the dark hole. There was loud popping, like hundreds of firecrackers going off, as the ladder smashed under Slow Bear's weight.

Jumping to his feet, Walker saw Gray Wolf and Silent Thunder on the ground fighting. The fallen torch gleamed nearby. First Gray Wolf was on top, then Silent Thunder. A knife was wedged between the four hands and two bodies.

Walker searched the flickering shadows of the plaza. Were No Name and Small Cub still in the village or had they gotten out? Where should he start to look?

*If only I could see—see where the boys are!*

"Small Cub!" Walker cried in frustration, waited a second, and repeated his loud call. The grunts, growls, and curses of the fight vibrated against his cries.

*Taawa, help me!*

Walker rushed up to one of the hide-draped doors that opened up into the plaza. He threw back the coarse hide. "Small Cub!"

Frightened female gasps came from within the dark room. Walker ran to the next house and the next, pulling up the door coverings and calling. The seconds flashed by.

Barking, Dog rushed through the village's open entrance. Something white flopped up and down around Dog's neck as she rushed toward Walker.

*Small Cub's shell pendant!* The boys had escaped.

He sprinted across the narrow plaza. Dog followed. The sounds of the life-and-death battle died with a blood-curdling scream. Walker ran through the entrance without a backward glance.

Walker started down the hill, leaving the village of tragedy behind. Whose death cry had he heard? Silent Thunder's or Gray Wolf's? It didn't really matter. Both men were his enemies—his people's enemies. Each man's heart was greedy to control the lives of others for his own gain. What was important now was to find the boys, avoid Silent Thunder's men, and get back to Lomaki as fast as possible.

*Lomaki.* Fear pumped through Walker. Was anyone still alive there? Or had Silent Thunder's men *finished it all?*

At the bottom of the hill, Dog made a sharp right turn and ran toward a steep cinder hill that silhouetted the moonlit horizon nearby. Walker followed, watching for Black Spider and Tangled Grass. Nothing moved. Even in the light of the full moon, he couldn't see very far, but then neither could Silent Thunder's men. Dog disappeared up the cinder hill.

The loose cinders and rocks made climbing up the steep hill treacherous. Bending forward, Walker scrambled up on all fours, scraping the skin off his knees. He couldn't see or hear Dog, but he didn't dare whistle or call out.

From the top of the cinder hill, all Walker could see were the dim outlines of more cinder hills and endless darkness. Crunching down to keep from being seen, he tried to catch his breath, which tore at his lungs like white fire. Where were Dog and the boys? If only he could *see* them. He shut his eyes and tried to see through the self-imposed darkness of his mind.

Nothing came, but below him there was the sound of rolling rocks. Walker's eyes flew open, and he slid down toward the sound, seeing nothing before him or in his mind.

The hill became studded with large rocks that graduated into huge boulders. Walker wove in and around them, searching. Did he dare call? Where were Silent Thunder's men? Time was running out. How long would it take the victor of the fight to come searching for him? Neither Gray Wolf nor Silent Thunder would let him get away if they could help it.

"Walker." The words sounded like the winter wind's song.

Whirling around, Walker saw a dark space between two boulders. Dog rushed out of the opening that was too little for an adult but perfect for a child to squeeze into. No Name and Small Cub followed.

Walker hugged the boys to him. He felt Small Cub's slender body trembling, while No Name held himself rigid. "Are you both okay?"

"Yes," No Name's confident voice answered.

"Have you seen Silent Thunder's two men?"

"They passed by us just after we hid. I think they were circling back to the village," No Name whispered. "They were grumbling about not being near a warm fire."

They would be out again if Silent Thunder was still alive. What if Gray Wolf had won? Would they kill him, or would they join his ranks?

"You must come to Lomaki with us, No Name," Walker said.

The boy arched his back and jerked away. "No Name is what Silent Thunder called me. My name is Strong Heart."

"A name you have honored." Walker touched his bony shoulder. "Strong Heart, our people would be proud to have you join us."

Strong Heart's back straightened, and his shoulder's squared. "I know a way to Lomaki that even Silent Thunder's men won't follow." He started down the hill. Dog ran at his heels.

"Can Strong Heart really live with us?" Small Cub asked, still clinging to Walker.

"Yes, wherever our people go." Walker wondered why Strong Heart had stayed so long under Silent Thunder's vicious rule. Just from what he had seen tonight, he was sure Strong Heart could have escaped long ago.

*Silent Thunder owns people in every village . . . His power is everywhere.* The words came back to Walker as he took Small Cub's hand and started after Strong Heart, who was halfway down the hill. There was no place the boy could have gone, Walker realized.

The minutes raced by like seconds yet dragged like

decades as the three moved across a huge, flat cinder field. Walker was not sure where they were, but Strong Heart seemed to know. Clouds had moved across much of the sky, blocking out many of its twinkling guideposts. At times even the moon's rays were hidden, yet Strong Heart kept moving as if led by an inner compass.

The cold night air raised goosebumps on Walker's neck, while sweat covered his chest and forehead. He was carrying Small Cub piggyback now. His legs were cramping, and his back ached, and the rest of his body screamed for rest. How long had it been since they had left Silent Thunder's village? Walker asked himself. He had no idea, but he kept moving, one foot in front of the other. How much farther was it to Lomaki? He wished he knew exactly where they were. Were they being followed and by whom? Unanswerable questions streaked back and forth in his mind as his feet pounded the cinders.

Strong Heart stopped with a jerk and whirled around just as they crested a steep summit. In the moonlight, Walker could see his tenseness. "Over this ridge," his breath came in even huffs, "is the canyon of the two hearted—the witches. When my grandfather's grandfather was young, witches lived there—witches that ate the flesh of others."

Walker's scalp prickled. A frigid wind blew up out of the canyon. Small Cub's arms tightened around his neck in a death grip.

"Are the witches still there?" Small Cub asked.

"It is said that their spirits still live there. No one goes into the canyon."

"You have, though." Walker looked down at Strong Heart. His face was pale in the moonlight.

"Just once, when the sun was bright. The canyon is small with very steep, rocky walls on all sides, but there is a way to go through. On the other side is a fast way to Lomaki."

Small Cub's arms tightened even more. "Walker, look!"

Swinging around, Walker saw a flickering torch light moving across the cinder field below them.

"Walker, will they stop following us," Small Cub's voice was as cold as the night, "if we go into the . . ."

"I don't know." Walker shifted Small Cub's weight and started down into the unknown darkness of the witches' canyon.

# 15

From what Walker could see in the bright moonlight, he realized Witches' Canyon was a huge natural sink rather than a canyon. He had a vivid image of the rocky ground opening up like a giant drain and the earth around it being sucked downward like water disappearing down a bathtub drain. A shiver slithered up his back. Had the gods been so appalled at the witches' sinful practices that they had caused the earth to open up and swallow all their wickedness?

Walker couldn't judge the actual size of the sink, but its sides were almost vertical. Small Cub was no longer on his back. With one hand, Walker held Small Cub's hand, helping him down, over, and around the rocky ledges. It was all he could do to keep Small Cub and himself upright.

Strong Heart led the way but was less certain of his directions now. More than once he had had to stop to search for a path among the rocks. "I think it's this way," he mumbled.

*Taawa, guide us to safety,* Walker prayed silently.

Angry voices from above whipped down in the wind. "Witches . . . "

"Silent Thunder . . . bring back or die . . . "

Looking up at the rim, Walker saw the torchlight dancing against the dark sky. He heard bits and pieces of the men's argument as he tried to go faster.

"Spirits . . . "

"Fool . . . "

"Witches . . . "

"Coward . . . "

"We are just about at the bottom of the canyon," Strong Heart said over his shoulder.

The ground evened out. Walker hunched down. "Small Cub, hop back on my back."

Small Cub's bony ribs knocked against Walker's back as Walker sprinted across the narrow floor of the sink. Strong Heart and Dog pressed ahead.

"Walker, the light is coming down into the canyon," Small Cub cried.

Walker lengthened his stride. "Keep watching it for me."

A cloud slid over the moon. Strong Heart moved back and forth along the opposite side of the sink with Dog pacing beside him. "I can't find the path up!"

Small Cub clung tighter to Walker. "The light is halfway down the side."

"We'll make our own trail." Walker started up between two huge boulders, slipped on the cinders, caught himself, and pushed on. Dog raced ahead. Moonlight filtered out from the edges of a cloud as it drifted in the night sky. Walker couldn't see any kind of path but continued working up, around, and over the rocks and boulders. Small Cub's grip became tighter. A sheer wall of rock stopped him cold.

"There is a path leading up and over this wall," Strong Heart said from behind. "Everything looks so different in the moonlight, but I think it is to the right."

"They're at the foot of the canyon," Small Cub reported, as Walker moved along the base of the wall. "Now they're crossing the floor of the canyon. They're running!"

"They are afraid, afraid of witches," Strong Heart's voice was defiant.

Walker knelt down. "Small Cub, climb off. We'll have to scale the wall." He heard a whooshing sound, as if air was being sucked in and swallowed by the cliff behind them. Small Cub's arm flew back around Walker's neck.

"Spirits!"

Walker pried Small Cub's arms from his neck. "Not spirits," Walker sputtered. His vocal cords felt smashed. Both boys stood inches from him, trembling.

Dog went ahead sniffing the rock wall. Within a foot, she came to an abrupt stop, growling. Walker got to his feet. "Hush!" He took Small Cub's hand and moved toward the animal. The sucking sound grew louder. Walker felt air rushing over his stockingless feet.

Moonlight washed over the cliff as the clouds slipped away from the moon. A ragged-edged gap stared out from the wall. Walker reached his hand toward it. The fracture was gulping in air. Small Cub pulled back.

"It's okay. It must be a blowhole of some kind." The dark space wasn't as tall as Walker and was only two and half feet across. "It looks more like a cave." Walker let go of Small

Cub's hand and stepped up to the dark crevice. "It *is* a cave. Stay here."

As Walker squeezed in sideways, total darkness met his eyes. He could feel air being sucked in from the outside. Carefully, with his hands out in front, he followed the air flow for six or seven steps. His hands touched rough rock. Walker ran his hands along the wall downward to the floor. The sucking became stronger. At the base of the wall, Walker felt the curbed edges of a hole and air rushing into it. He felt around the smooth opening. It seemed to be about as big as a man's head. "It is a blowhole!" Walker stated, trying to calm his own fears.

Back in the future, when his class had visited Wupatki National Monument, a park ranger had explained blowholes as they had stood by the large hole near Wupatki Ruins. Walker tried to remember what the ranger had said. Bits and pieces came to mind. Blowholes were openings in the earth that were connected to deep, natural cracks or tunnels in the ground. Air was either blown out or sucked into these openings depending on the earth's temperature and the air pressure.

Hadn't the ranger said that the area had a good number of these blowholes? Walker dredged his memory. Yes, but nothing had been said about any blowholes being found in caves. Maybe no one in the future had discovered this unusual one. Perhaps in the seven hundred years that had passed, it had been destroyed by an earthquake or something. Walker's thoughts raced. He tugged his mind back to the present. The boys could hide here. He would lead the two men away and find a way to deal with them somehow.

Walker started to move toward the entrance of the cave,

but his outstretched hands felt a solid wall again. In the total darkness, his sense of direction had been distorted. His heart raced as a wave of fear built within him. He'd give anything for his flashlight right now! Why had he given it to Tag to take instead of keeping it? Sidestepping, and with his hands reading the rough rock like braille, Walker inched along the wall. As long as the cave wasn't too large, he'd be able to find the entrance fairly fast, he reasoned, trying to keep calm.

*Please Taawa, let me . . .*

Walker tripped over something on the floor of the cave. Brittle crunching and crackling filled the cave as he landed. Something gored into his ribs and hip. Pushing himself up, his fingers felt something round in shape. It was hard, dry, and rough. Panic clamped down on Walker. His scalp tightened and tingled. Walker yanked his hand away and tried to get up. With each movement there were more cracks and snaps. His other hand touched something tubular in shape. It felt thinner in the middle, fatter towards its rounded ends.

Walker was somewhere beyond terror, as he forced his mind to work logically. *Bones—just dried up old bones,* he told himself getting to a standing position. *But whose?*

"Walker, they're coming!" Strong Heart's words came through the darkness.

Walker moved toward the words. "Keep talking, Strong Heart."

The boy's words were a harsh whisper. "They're starting up this side of the canyon."

Walker encountered three or four more piles of bones before he felt the cool air being sucked in through the cave's entrance. Just inside the entrance way, Walker again turned and stared into the terrifying blackness.

Shell Listener's words thundered in Walker's mind. *Darkness—darkness broken by the whiteness of bones . . . Strike these together. They shall light the darkness and protect you.*

Walker fumbled with the knot on his waist pouch. Driving his hand into the leather bag, he brought out the two smooth stones Shell Listener had given to him. He manipulated the cylinder shaped rocks until the smaller one nested in the longitudinal trough of the larger one. Pulling, them apart, he banged them together.

Nothing.

Walker tried again, this time harder. An eerie, whitish glow began to slowly emanate from both stones. Startled, Walker almost dropped them. His mind searched for a logical explanation to the glowing—some kind of electrical charge caused by the rushing air in the cave or a high iron content within the walls of the cave. Perhaps the . . .

"Walker, where are you?" Small Cub's voice was desperate.

Closing his hands around the stones, Walker squeezed through the cave's narrow entrance. Strong Heart, Small Cub, and Dog stood rooted where he had left them. Walker could see the flickering of the torch threading through the rocks below them. It would be only a matter of minutes before Tangled Grass and Black Spider followed their tracks up here. With the torch they had the advantage—or did they? Walker squeezed the stones.

"Small Cub, Strong Heart," Walker knelt between the boys. Their faces were washed in moonlight and fear. "We have a chance, but you both must be very brave, braver than you have ever been before in your lives." Walker could hear rocks dislodged by the two men rolling down the canyon side.

"You must trust in Taawa to protect and help us." Walker felt the boys' fear. "We must hide in the cave. You must be brave because the bones of others have their resting place within the cave."

Small Cub gasped and cried at the same time. Walker squeezed his shoulder. "The spirits of those resting here are friendly. They will help us." He prayed he was telling the truth.

"Dog must hide, too," Strong Heart said with determination, though he trembled in Walker's arm.

Walker moved to the mouth of the cave, guiding the boys. "Yes, but we must hurry." He opened his hand. The stones were all but dark. Walker struck them together again with a hard whack.

"Lightning stones," Strong Heart said in amazement as the eerie light began to glow.

Inside the cave, even with the rocks glowing, darkness permeated everywhere. Walker led the way, holding the rocks out in front of him for what light they gave. He held Small Cub's hand with his other hand. Strong Heart completed the chain, holding on to Small Cub, with Dog at his heels. The nearer they got to the blowhole, the brighter the rocks' light grew.

"Small Cub, you lie here, on your stomach. Keep your eyes closed. Try not to breathe. They must think that the witches killed us, too. Just remember the spirits here are friendly." Walker helped ease the boy down in about what he thought was the center of cave. He felt Small Cub's body shaking. "I know you can do it."

"Where will you be?"

"Right in front of you. Strong Heart and Dog will be right

on the other side of you." Walker noticed that the stones were dimming again. Timing was going to be crucial. He smacked the stones together. In the dim glow he could make out Strong Heart pulling Dog down next to him on the ground near Small Club. He was glad that the stones didn't light the cave enough for the boys to see the white remains strewn around the cave's edges.

"Good, Strong Heart. Lie on your stomach, with Dog behind you. Hold her down, and muzzle her if you have to." Walker carefully made his way to the blowhole. He stooped down and followed the wall until he reached the first set of bones.

Black Spider's harsh voice echoed outside. "They couldn't have just disappeared! Look for more tracks."

Walker's hands were wet as he probed the pile of bones. He easily recognized a long leg bone by its shape and length. Pushing it aside, he found a much smaller bone. He could feel small nicks, like teeth marks on it. Strong Heart's statement about the witches eating the flesh of others exploded in Walker's mind. Fighting down the fear and nausea, Walker pushed aside the gnawed bone and continued searching.

"Here are their tracks." Tangled Grass's voice sounded like it was within a few feet of the cave.

*Taawa, forgive us for disturbing this resting place.* Before Walker could finish his silent prayer, he felt what he was searching for. Trying not to think about what he was holding, Walker worked his way back to where Small Cub lay.

"I am here, little brothers," he whispered lying next to the boys. "Just keep your eyes closed."

Black Spider's voice broke through the darkness of the cave. "Here are their tracks."

The entrance of the cave got brighter as the flickering torchlight came closer. Walker hit the rocks together with a loud crack and slipped a glowing stone into each of the oval-shaped eyesockets of the skull he held. They fit almost perfectly, as if they had been made for just this purpose. Walker's blood was ice. He lay down on his back and draped one arm over Small Cub and felt him shaking. "It is okay," Walker whispered. With his other hand, he placed the skull on his chest. Its eyes glowed toward the entrance. The air being pulled into the blowhole rushed over Walker, sucking his breath with it.

*Be with us now, Great Taawa.*

The entrance of the cave lit up with flickering brightness.

# 16

Flickering shadows danced inside the small cave from the torch outside its entrance. Walker's heart thundered in his ears. He could now see the drifts of white bones scattered around the dark edges of the cave. He fought down the bile rising in his throat and told himself that there was more to fear from the two men outside the cave than from the skeletal remains that lay nearby.

Black Spider's voice carried into the cave. "They have to be in there."

"Come out!" Tangled Grass sounded more frightened than demanding.

Dog growled.

"What was that?"

"They're just trying to scare us off." The cave exploded into swaying light as the torch was thrust inside the entrance. Walker fought to keep his eyes open, not blinking, just staring straight ahead with the vacant look of death.

Black Spider's crouched, pudgy body squeezed in after the torch. He straightened and took a step inside the cave. The blowhole's rushing air sucked at the torch's flame, drawing it toward the back of the cave. Ghostly fingers of light spread through the small, rocky recess.

The man's face drained as he gaped at the three lifeless boys surrounded by the harsh whiteness of scattered bones. His large mouth flopped open, but no sound came out. The torch's flame was drawn stronger by the blowhole's sucking air.

Tangled Grass's pocked face and thin shoulders appeared through the entrance. In a breath's time, he scrutinized the site of flesh and bones. His scream of terror rang through the cave as he escaped through its opening. The canyon walls echoed with his shrieks until they died in the distance.

The cave went pitch black as the blowhole's gulping air finally extinguished Black Spider's torch. From the corner of his eye, Walker could see the light coming from the skull on his chest. He heard a whining gasp, the sound of the torch pole hitting the ground, followed by Black Spider's desperate struggle to get out of the cave's narrow entrance.

Small Cub squirmed under Walker's arm. Walker pressed down to keep him still. Dog growled. Black Spider wailed. It sounded as if he fell face first out of the cave. The noise of his running feet died seconds later. The cold air rushing in, over, and around the bones of the living and the dead was the only noise in witch's cave.

A chuckle started to build in Walker's chest and grew to roaring laughter that bounced around the small cave. He felt Small Cub's leather-clad body trembling under his arm. Walker sat up, pulled Small Cub close, and hugged him.

"Nothing to fear but fear itself," he could barely get the future-famous words out between the waves of laughter that now wracked his body, releasing all his pent-up tension and fear.

Small Cub pulled away. Walker fought to control the laughter that was bringing tears to his eyes. "It's all right, little brothers. You did it! Both of you were unbelievably brave!" Walker got to his feet, anxious to leave the remains in the cave to their endless sleep.

"Will they tell Silent Thunder that we are dead?" Small Cub asked as they made their way over the rim of the sink.

Walker followed Strong Heart down the ridge. "I hope so. Silent Thunder would have no reason to hunt for us then. We can get our people and leave before the sun rises." Even with his hopeful words, worry stabbed deep into Walker's mind. The rest of Silent Thunder's men had had all night *to finish it all*. He had to face the possibly that there might not be anyone left alive at Lomaki.

Walker's tired legs got weaker, shakier. Once Black Spider and Tangled Grass made it back to Silent Thunder with their report, a final execution order would surely be given, if anyone was still alive at Lomaki. Nothing would stop Silent Thunder if he thought Walker was dead. Would Silent Thunder even order Flute Maiden to be . . .

"It's not far to Lomaki now," Strong Heart's confident words broke through Walker's turmoil. "Once we get down this ridge, we cross a flat area and then drop down to your village."

"I owe you much, Strong Heart. Without your courage, we would be in Masau'u's hands right now. Kwa kwa."

Walker saw Strong Heart's back become straighter and felt a new sense of pride in him.

The moon hung in the west as they crossed the large, open cinder field. Small Cub was on Walker's back, with his head resting on Walker's shoulders. Strong Heart was leading the way. Walker was amazed at the boy's endurance. His own throat felt like sandpaper. His legs were tight with fatigue and strain. His body screamed for rest.

*Taawa, be with my people,* Walker prayed as he pushed on.

Lomaki stood silently in the shadows of the clouds and moonlight as the three hid behind the crest of a cinder hill overlooking the dark village.

"Stay here with Strong Heart and Dog." Walker stooped and slid Small Cub off his back. "Watch the roof for my signal."

Small Cub started to protest.

Walker cut him off. "Strong Heart, if no signal comes, go to Leaning Tree's village. Take Small Cub with you. Ask Leaning Tree for help."

Trying to keep out of sight, Walker made his way down the hill and toward the village. He climbed down the east side of the earth crack, using its rocks and ledges as cover. Walker waited until a cloud covered the moon and then sprinted across the narrow floor of the gully and into the rocks on the opposite side. As the moon slipped out from behind the cloud, Lomaki stood on the ledge above him—silent and still.

Walker climbed up the rocky wall, edged himself over the rim, and lay flat on the ground, inches from the outside wall of the village. Silence danced in the air. He scooted around to the entrance. The thick stone slab stood strong and tight in the doorway. Relief flooded over him. "Scar Cheek, Son of Great Bear."

"Walker!" Scar Cheek answered from above. The scraping sound of the ladder being lowered over the roof broke through the tense darkness.

"Is everyone safe?"

Scar Cheek helped Walker over the rooftop. "Yes, there were noises but we . . . "

Someone grabbed Walker's arm and jerked him around. "Small Cub—did you find Small Cub?" Son of Great Bear demanded.

"He is waiting on the hill." Son of Great Bear's hand dropped away from Walker's arm. *Where did Son of Great Bear stand in regard to Silent Thunder?* Walker knew there wasn't time to sort it all out. "We must leave now."

"We just can't . . . "

Walker locked eyes with Son of Great Bear. "If we don't leave now, Silent Thunder won't let us live till sunset." Son of Great Bear's face drained white in the moonlight.

Movement came from behind them. Morning Flower and Flute Maiden appeared on the inner ladder. They hurried to Son of Great Bear with their questions. In a rush, the others emerged onto the rooftop. They clustered around Walker. Anxiety, fear, and unasked questions swirled in the air.

Walker looked around at the frightened faces—Scar Cheek, Arrow Maker, Fawn, Morning Flower, and all the others. He loved each as his family. How could he leave *anyone* behind? But just as it had been at Walnut Canyon, he couldn't force them to come. If only there was time to explain things fully and answer questions—but there wasn't. Each minute they stayed, the closer Silent Thunder and his men could come. Those who trusted him would leave. Those who did not would face Silent Thunder.

Walker's eyes sought Flute Maiden. Her downcast face was hidden in the shadows of those around her. If only he could speak to her alone and explain what Silent Thunder really wanted . . . Doubt clouded Walker's thoughts. Would Flute Maiden's heart allow her mind to believe him?

Shaking his head, Walker focused on the immediate need. "We must leave. There is no time to explain, except that Lomaki has been marked for death, not by the dead but by the living. We must leave as soon as we can gather what we can carry."

\* \* \*

As the sun reached its warming fingers over the horizon, it found the band almost halfway to the Little Colorado River north of Lomaki. Walker led the group, with Strong Heart and Dog at his side. Scar Cheek took up the rear position of the small, tight group. Walker had pushed as fast as the others could go. Now in the early morning light, without night's shroud to cover them, he felt death searing at their heels.

With each step, Walker battled to keep his sleep-deprived mind thinking good thoughts, positive thoughts, but his heart fought to relive the last hurried minutes at Lomaki. Each incident, distorted with Walker's weariness, played through his mind's eye over and over again as his feet trudged forward. He felt the joy, shadowed by anxiety, as he remembered the moment Morning Flower and Son of Great Bear embraced Small Cub. Walker had slipped away then. He didn't have the emotional strength or the time to discuss whether Son of Great Bear intended to stay or leave.

His mind skipped to his brief discussion with Scar Cheek. Oh-ay, Scar Cheek and his family would leave with Walker. Again, yes, Scar Cheek would take up the rear position, in a sense agreeing to share leadership responsibility. Where the meeting had taken place and what exactly had been said was washed into the shadows of Walker's fatigue. Only the feeling of gratitude for Scar Cheek's support was clear as Walker's memory changed to the final, nightmarish minutes at Lomaki.

A tight throng of people huddled together in the small entrance room of the village. The anxious faces, bodies, bundles, and huge baskets melted together in the darkness. Fear filled the tight room. Walker couldn't see Son of Great Bear's family or Flute Maiden. A lump clogged his throat. He swallowed hard. "Scar Cheek, help me with the slab."

The people streamed out but kept in a tight knot of bodies. Walker took his position in the front and set out. Cinders crunching echoed behind him. The sound of the slab being drug across the Lomaki's entrance reached Walker's ears. His feet stumbled. Who was staying behind? Through a veil of tears, Walker focused his eyes straight ahead, and forced his feet to keep plowing through the cinders.

In the dark hours following, Walker had not allowed himself to look back and count those who followed. Now, some five miles away from Lomaki, with the sun on the eastern horizon, Walker still had not taken a tally of who had come and who had stayed behind. The bright sunlight bleached out the dark memories playing in his mind. Walker forced his concentration onto the situation at hand. "Will Silent Thunder come after us, Strong Heart?" he asked, clutching his spear tighter as they plodded on.

"You and your people were a threat to him at Lomaki."
Strong Heart shifted the water jug on his shoulder. "Silent
Thunder is hungry to control all the villages—their trade,
farmland, and people. There is nothing on the other side of
the river for him except lizards and snakes. He has no reason
to follow once we cross the river." Without missing a step,
Strong Heart looked Walker straight in the eye. "Unless there
is something else he wants that you have."

Coldness numbed Walker's mind. Did he still have the
one thing Silent Thunder had obviously wanted?

## 17

Walker stared down into the rugged Little Colorado Gorge, as it would be named someday in the future. A thread-thin stream wound through the narrow canyon floor below. It was this scant water that had kept his people alive at Lomaki during the past months. Now it and its steep abyss seemed to be the unofficial boundary that separated them from Silent Thunder's death squad. As yet, there had been no sign of anyone following. Walker knew that Silent Thunder's men would be able to travel like lightning compared to his own group of men, women, and children, each burdened with large baskets, heavy water jugs, canteens, bows, arrows, spears, and other essentials.

The San Francisco Peaks now rose above the horizon on the other side of the canyon. White clouds, edged in tones of gray, gathered around the three high peaks of the mountain. Were the Kachinas, the Hopis' guardian spirits who lived on *Nuvatukya'ovi*, watching over them? Walker hoped so, because

Masau'u would stalk his people with hunger, thirst, cold, and exhaustion every step of the way to Hopi. Walker preferred taking his chances against the god of death, who was bound by the laws of nature, rather than Silent Thunder, who broke all of the gods' laws.

"We'll push on, even though I doubt anyone will be able to track us once they get to the river," Walker told Scar Cheek, who stood close by, watching the opposite side of the canyon for movement. The others rested about fifty feet away. Walker's weary mind still refused to recognize any one person. The clustered group was just a blur of bodies without faces.

"My feet are still cold from walking in the water," Scar Cheek replied. "It is lucky that the water was so low, or we couldn't have walked so far in it."

*The oldest trick on television,* Walker thought. They had traveled in the river eastward, crisscrossing the stream on rocks and wading in the water for at least three miles. There was no safe way up through the sheer cliffs at that point, so they again returned to the water. After a few more miles, they had finally climbed out of the gorge, following a faint animal trail that wrapped around and over the steep, rocky ledges. Scar Cheek swept the path with boughs of sagebrush. It would appear to anyone following them that the river had just swallowed all of them up in one giant gulp.

Walker picked up the basket of dried fish, meat, and cornmeal he was carrying. "I just hope it all works." He slung the basket over his aching shoulder, along with his bow and water jug, and looked at the sun, which now hung midway in the western sky. Walker knew the others were tired, too, especially the children, but they had to keep going. "At dusk we'll find some kind of shelter for the night." As his ears heard his own words, his body cried out in rebellion. How could he go another step without sleep? Would the tight web of fatigue ever leave his mind, so he could have the physical and emotional strength to actually see who had stayed behind? The deep, instinctive drive to keep moving controlled his every thought and movement.

"Walker," Quiet Wind said from behind. "We'll stay behind to watch for anyone following. If anyone is following, this is the place to stop them."

Resistance started to form in Walker's mind.

"Go. We'll catch up with you later," Scar Cheek.

Walker nodded, too tired to argue, and started walking. The others fell in place behind him.

As the sky began to grow dark, it appeared that a wind-painted hill of brilliant pink, dark green, and gray sand was the only possible shelter. By this time, Walker's mind was an exhausted haze. The second wind of energy that had carried his body since crossing the river was now spent.

Scar Cheek and Quiet Wind had just caught up with the group again. "Walker, sleep. I'm sure no one is following us, but we'll post a watch on the top of the hill and take care of everything else," Scar Cheek said, helping Walker ease the heavy basket off his shoulder.

Walker sank to his knees. "Be sure Strong Heart and Dog get enough to eat," he forced out the words as he burrowed into the warm, soft sand. Sleep, with its comforting darkness, came even before he shut his eyes.

In the shadowy night, coldness seeped into Walker's bones. He tried to curl his body tighter, but the painful stiffness of his legs and arms stopped him. Walker's teeth chattered, and his body shivered. Exhaustion choked his aching body. Sleep gripped his mind.

Soft warmth drifted over Walker. He pried his eyes open a crack. Against the dimness of the stars, he saw a thin figure kneeling over him. He struggled to keep his eyes open, but sleep dragged him downward. Downy softness of turkey feathers tickled his neck. Walker managed to force his eyes open again. A shadowy face—Flute Maiden—hovered over him.

Had it been a dream or a vision? Walker wondered hours later as his mind drifted in and out of consciousness. Sleep clung to his eyes and shadowed his mind. How could it have been Flute Maiden? He hadn't seen her or her family since Lomaki, or had he? All that his mind had registered was the urgency to keep walking—the need to escape. Confusion clouded his drowsy mind.

Walker tried to roll over, but became tangled in the turkey blanket. He forced open his eyes. The sky was soft blue-gray in the chilly, early-morning light. Something moved behind him.

*Silent Thunder!* Walker flipped over as his hand flew to his knife. He jerked up. His feet were snagged in the folds of the blanket, and he stumbled backward into the soft sand.

Flopping over, he saw Flute Maiden a few feet away. Her startled look was replaced with a shy smile.

"I'm sorry. I didn't mean to scare you," her voice matched her smile. She moved closer.

Walker untangled himself from the blanket, keeping his eyes down. His cheeks felt hot.

Flute Maiden knelt down to face him. She touched his hand. "I—we must talk."

Beneath the tears shimmering in Flute Maiden's eyes,

Walker saw something he hadn't seen in the long months at Lomaki. Had his jealousy blinded him to what Flute Maiden's eyes now reflected?

"Deer!" a hoarse whisper came from the top of the sand dune. Walker snatched up his bow and started to climb the dune. Others on both sides of him scrambled up in a mass of arms, legs, bodies, and bows.

A large buck moved along some fifty yards below. Crouching down on the top of the dune, Walker looked around him. Scar Cheek, Arrow Maker, and Quiet Wind knelt to his left, their eyes following the slow-moving animal. To his right knelt Rising Sun and Son of Great Bear, both easing arrows into their bows. *All* of his people had followed him and Taawa had just provided fresh meat!

New determination surged over Walker. He knew that whatever problems needed to be worked out within the band would be handled. His people would stand together to fight against Masau'u and, if necessary, Silent Thunder. With Taawa's help they would endure and survive the long journey to the Hopi Mesas.

Walker crept down the sand dune, with the others fanning out around him. He wouldn't allow himself to think about the likelihood that the Hopi wouldn't let them stay on their land. Right now, in the light of a new day, everything seemed too hopeful, too positive, to think about that very real possibility.

\* \* \*

"We'll stretch the deer hide between these two sturdy branches to make a pole sled," Walker explained as he used his knife to cut away the smaller limbs off a thick juniper branch. Small Cub and Strong Heart squatted nearby watching. The sounds of the others setting up camp for the night carried in the evening breeze. After five days of traveling without a sign of being followed, the band had settled into a nightly routine.

Strong Heart looked doubtful. Morning Flower had cut his long bangs so his eyes looked even larger than before. "The branches are too scrawny and dry. They will snap."

"Not if we spread the weight around," Walker glanced up. "It will hold what little weight Dog can pull." He felt lucky to even have found a tree, weathered as it was, in the barren terrain they hiked that day.

Small Cub patted Dog's head. "She's so strong, she could pull a whole big bear." Dog wagged her tail. "See, she even says so."

"I hope we don't meet any bears along the way." Walker winked at Strong Heart, who smiled back. "But it will help if Dog can pull a few pounds of weight."

"We can put Small Light on the sled instead of in her cradle board." Small Cub fingered the first branch Walker had cropped smooth. "Small Light is little; she just cries big."

Strong Heart reached out and petted Dog. "And if Dog runs after a rabbit, your baby sister can use your hunting stick to kill it."

Before Small Cub could find a retort to the teasing, Scar Cheek approached. "The food is ready, boys." Both were up and running in an instant with Dog loping beside them.

Walker's stomach growled, but he kept shaving the second branch. Scar Cheek squatted beside him. "The women used the last of the deer meat. I wish we could have carried more." He picked up the finished pole and turned it over in his large, scarred hands.

Walker wondered again what kind of injury had caused the deep scar across his face and both hands as well. "With what food we were able to bring and what we can hunt and gather along the way, we'll be all right." Walker said, slashing the last twig off the pole. He didn't add he was more worried about water than food. Despite the cool to cold temperatures of late autumn, thirst was a constant traveling companion. They could cinch their belts tighter against hunger, but not against thirst. Even with every person, including the children, carrying water jugs or canteens and rationing every drop, the water from the Little Colorado River had lasted only three days. Amazingly, they had found a small spring the next day. Now with the water containers on the low side again, Walker had begun to worry.

"I would rather face stomach hunger than live under Silent Thunder's spirit-starved rule," Scar Cheek stated, standing.

Walker slipped his knife into his belt and examined the two poles. He had discussed Silent Thunder with the rest of the people and remembered the pained look on Flute Maiden's face as Strong Heart described Silent Thunder's cruelty to the women and children of his village. Son of Great Bear had just stared into space as Walker explained Silent Thunder's economical and political control over the Wupatki area.

During the strenuous walk each day, Son of Great Bear stayed aloof from the others, even Morning Flower and his children. Walker sensed that he was trying to come to terms with himself. He had not spoken to Walker since leaving Lomaki.

Walker sighed at the thought. Someday he hoped they could talk freely again; he missed Son of Great Bear's friendship. Picking up the two sled poles, Walker stood. "I think we have seen the last of Silent Thunder and his men."

The image of Silent Thunder's angry face streaked across Walker's sight. *Find them. Find them and bring back the medicine woman!* Silent Thunder's words spoken many miles away reached through to Walker's mind.

# 18

A single eagle feather bound to a strand of cotton cordage was planted at the edge of the small spring near the base of an unusual rock butte. The feather danced in the cool breeze, twisting and swaying in humble thanks to the water providers.

Each time the water containers had been nearly empty, somehow a water source had been found. This was the first spring that had been marked by a prayer feather, though.

"It is a breath feather," Walker said, holding a jug in the cold water to fill it. The others had already satisfied their thirst, filled their water containers, and now were resting in the shadow of the tall butte. Walker and Scar Cheek knelt beside the shallow spring, letting the life-giving water seep into their water jugs. Seeing the questioning look on Scar Cheek's face, Walker continued. "My uncle told me stories about springs that continually run cold and sweet, that are watched over by holy beings." But he had thought Náat's stories, told so far in the future, were just legends repeated and recited generation after generation. Walker pulled his jug out of the water. Legends that were obviously true, he thought as he leaned the water jug up against a rock and began filling his small ceramic canteen.

Small Cub flopped down beside Walker. "Tell me the story."

"There are sweet springs at the foot of the Hopi mesas where the Hopi get their water," Walker began. "Sometimes, when the people are not living in harmony with each other or in balance with the world around them, these springs dry up. You see, where much is given, much is expected." Walker checked his canteen to see if was full yet. It wasn't, so he laid it back into the water.

"When a spring dries up, the Hopi start looking inward, asking what they are doing to cause the imbalance. They also seek the help of the water priest. This holy man prepares himself through fasting, prayer, and sacred rituals in the kiva. Then early one morning, with all the clan members praying, the water priest goes on a long and dangerous journey, seeking an eternal spring just like this one. If the prayers and rituals have been performed in the correct manner and spirit, the priest is led by the holy spirits to a spring with sweet, cold water."

"Like this one," Small Cub interjected, trailing his fingers in the water.

"Yes," Walker took his full canteen out of the water and placed the wooden stopper in its narrow opening at the top. "When the priest finds such a spring, he fills a sacred water jar, called a transplanter jar, with the sweet water. He also puts a prayer feather, a bit of moss, and any water bugs he sees into the jug. After the jug is full, the priest takes a special eagle feather, whispers a prayer of thanks on it, and plants it next to the spring as an offering to the spirit that owns the water."

Scar Cheek and Small Cub stared toward the lone eagle feather fluttering nearby. "Then what?" Small Cub asked.

"The water priest must run all the way back to his village, never setting down the transplanter jar, with its borrowed water, for even an instant."

"Why?" Small Cub inched closer.

"Wherever the transplanter jar is set down, all the essence of water is transferred to that very spot. So the priest can set the jar down only in the failing spring."

Small Cub plunged his hand into the shimmering pool and brought a handful of water out. It ran through his fingers, returning to the spring. "The priest must be a very good runner."

"Only the strongest runners can become water priests," Walker said. "The priest half buries the jar in the dying spring while saying holy prayers. As long as the transplanter jar is not touched or removed and everything has been done in the correct manner, the spring will be renewed and the Hopi's thirst satisfied, just as ours has been."

Walker watched the nearby eagle feather swaying and dancing. The feather didn't appear very old, perhaps six or seven moons. With the Hopi's springs drying up, what were the chances that they would let Walker and his people share their limited water? Walker prayed that the water priest's crusade had been successful.

"It should be only a few more days," Walker said, looking at the others huddled around the small fire. The night air was bitter cold. The stars had the sky to themselves. Walker had decided to camp near the spring, so everyone could drink deeply of its water and rest their tired bodies.

The smell of roasted rabbit cut through the campfire smoke. Since there had been no signs of anyone following, the band now used a well-concealed fire each night to cook and warm themselves. The threat of Silent Thunder still nagged at Walker, but the bitter coldness of the nights outweighed it.

Walker's stomach growled as he watched Morning Flower remove a fist-size rock from the edge of the fire. Strips of leather protected her hands. She dropped the hot stone into a cooking basket, causing hissing steam to rise. The portions of stew would be small but enough to provide strength to go on.

Every day had been the same—just enough dried or fresh meat for energy but not enough to fill or satisfy. The small band traveled from sunrise to sunset. Walker had lost track of the number of days they had hiked; one day blended into the next. But they had traveled faster than Walker thought possible and without injury or sickness. He knew that the Kachinas were watching over and guiding them.

The women and children gathered anything edible along the way, and the men hunted. They supplemented their dried meat with rabbit, snake, lizard, beetles, and other bugs. Even these had been hard to find due to the coldness.

One day Small Cub and Strong Heart found and raided a rat's nest. Everyone shared the rat's stash of nuts and seeds. Walker smiled at the memory. The people were working as one again. They gave strength to and received it from one another every step of the way. Despite the cold, hearts were warmed with new harmony. The ghosts of the troubled days at Lomaki had faded.

Small Cub's voice brought Walker's mind back to the flickering fire and the star-studded night. "Do the boys at Hopi hunt rabbits?" he asked, toying with his wooden hunting stick that resembled a boomerang. Small Cub was sitting between Walker and Strong Heart. Flames popped and danced, licking the juice from the rabbit being turned on a spit.

Walker nodded. "Hopi boys use the same kind of hunting sticks as you do, but I doubt any boy your age is as skillful as you are."

"I'll be glad to teach them." Small Cub's face gleamed in the firelight.

"I am sure the Hopi boys are not as modest as you, either," Strong Heart teased. Everyone had welcomed him into the group and even found a pair of leather leggings and a tunic for him to wear against the cold. Dog was curled up next to him, dozing.

Small Cub crinkled his face. "Are the Hopi different from us?"

"The Hopi's ways and beliefs are a bit different, but they, too, seek peace and harmony within themselves and those around them. They also pray to Taawa for protection and guidance." Walker could see that everyone huddled around the fire was listening, as they had each night when he talked about the Hopi. In each face he saw fatigue mixed with worry about the future. Walker wished he could promise that once they reached Hopi, all the hunger, thirst, and hardships that they were enduring would end. But he couldn't. His constant prayer was that the hearts of their Hopi brothers would be softened toward them.

"Whatever we find at Hopi will be better than Lomaki." Flute Maiden's voice was low but firm. She looked across the fire toward Walker with a smile. The daily routine had left little time and energy for them to talk alone, but the few times they had, their words were from the heart. The wall of tension and misunderstanding that had been building between them was slowly crumbling.

"Lomaki wasn't haunted by the spirits of the dead but by the living," Son of Great Bear stated, gazing deep into the fire.

Walker studied him. He looked like his old self once more. His back was straight, his shoulder squared. He no longer seemed oppressed with an unseen burden. Great Bear had won the battle of regaining his inner peace, which had been shattered during the last days at Lomaki.

The long hours of walking day after day had given Walker plenty of time to analyze what had happened within himself also. He realized now that under the pressures and stress of being high chief, he, too, had changed, and not for the best in some ways. Jealousy and anger had clouded his heart and eyes, while authority, responsibility, and inner harmony were a constant tug-of-war within him. He wondered if he would ever find a balance or have the courage to use his inner sight.

Son of Great Bear's voice had a storytelling quality as he continued. "Lomaki and the villages all around it were once good places to grow corn and raise children. The people worked hard to live there." Every eye was upon him, every ear listening. "Then as the people began to prosper, their hearts grew selfish. Perhaps when life is too easy, then one wants more for less." Son of Great Bear held Walker's eye. "Greed is powerful, more powerful than love and self-honor."

* * *

"There on the tallest mesa," Walker said, pointing with his chin, "is the village of Oraibi."

Small Cub shaded his eyes. "I don't see anything."

"It's there on the very edge of the mesa. It's hard to see because its walls are made of rocks from the mesa. It's still a good day-and-a-half walk." He looked toward the east. Walker couldn't see the flat-topped mountain where his twentieth-century village would stand someday, but just coming back to the land where he been raised was enough. He recognized a few prominent land formations, though they were somewhat different. He was home!

The others gathered around Walker on the ridge. Excitement rippled the air. Husbands and wives talked. Children pressed for a better view. Strong Heart stood next to Small Cub. Dog sat in between them, thumping her tail in the dirt.

"The soil is almost red," Fawn said. Walker was sure she was thinking about clay for her pottery.

"At times, the undersides of the clouds are pink from the color of the land," Walker told her. Turning to Flute Maiden, he said, "I know that your healing skill will be needed, but I don't know where to find all the plants for your medicines."

She smiled. Her eyes searched the vista before her. "I'll learn where to find what I need. It is beautiful here and so big."

*Big enough for all of us*, thought Walker, though worry still gnawed at his heart. There were more than seven hundred years between these Hopi people and the Hopi with whom he had been raised. Things could be very different.

"If we plant our fields at the foot of the mesa," Scar

Cheek observed, "water will run off the mesa to water the corn, squash, and beans."

Rising Sun added, "There are many hills and ravines to use in the same way. The land goes on forever."

"Yes, but it is not our land." Son of Great Bear looked at Walker.

"That's true, but the traditions of Hopi are peaceful. They are waiting for the return of their brothers and sisters who were sent on sacred migrations after emerging from the sipapu into this, the fourth world."

"If they don't let us stay, where will we go?" Strong Heart asked.

The words lingered like ice forming in the cold.

*Where would we go?* Walker had no idea.

# 19

Each of my people brings skills that are valuable to your village." Walker kept his voice low, trying to keep out the nervousness that surged through him. He looked around the kiva at the Hopi clan leaders seated on the narrow stone bench that followed the side and back walls of the rectangular underground room. The walls were plastered white. Black and red designs and religious scenes were painted on them. Deep, shelf-like niches in the adobe walls held sacred items, most of which Walker recognized. A small fire in a clay-lined pit with a stone air deflector warmed the cold air. The pungent aroma of native tobacco blended with herbs and spice overpowered the smell of the fire's smoke. Wisps of white clouds from the many clay cloud blowers danced up the bright shaft of sunlight and out of the kiva's square roof entrance. Scar Cheek, Son of Great Bear, and Walker's other men sat at the back of the kiva, where the women typically sat during nonsecret ceremonials and meetings.

"Oh-ay, yes. Your people do have much to add to our village," said Winter Moon the Kikmongwi, village chief, of Oraibi. Smoke from his stubby, white ceramic pipe swirled up and around his gray hair. His dark, almond-shaped eyes dominated his round, deeply wrinkled face and reflected intelligence and kindness. As the other men in the kiva were, he was dressed in a simple tunic and leggings. His long, gray hair was tied at the nape of his neck, and straight bangs fell across his forehead. "We would be foolish not to welcome you into our village."

"My head and heart agree, but my stomach and those of our children do not." The harsh, raspy voice made Walker cringe. Circling Hawk stood up from where he sat. His back was just beginning to stoop with age, but his face was engraved with permanent scowl lines around his small mouth and narrow eyes. Gray highlighted his long, black hair. He was the warrior chief and a total contrast to Winter Moon. "Our storerooms have not been full for many seasons. Even the Kachinas have had little influence on the gods to bring rain to our crops. Our children's stomachs have growled for many winters." Circling Hawk took slow steps around the kiva. "They will cry with hunger even more if these people are allowed to stay. Oh-ay, they bring skills but no food!"

Walker saw nods of agreement. His hands were wet, his mouth dry. "Hunger is no stranger to my people. Our belts have been cinched against hunger for many seasons, too. My men and boys will hunt to help feed our people." Walker made eye contact with Winter Moon. "We do not want to be a strain on your village. We ask only to stay till the warmth returns to the mesas."

"Then where will you go?" Circling Hawk's direct question showed his disrespect. He stopped his migration around the room a few feet from Walker, his eyes narrowed.

"I am sure that you plant your crops in every possible spot around the village. But it is not wise to overburden Mother Earth in any one area with corn, squash, or beans. The soil becomes weak when it is overworked. The snows come so that Mother Earth can rest from her labors." Walker let his eyes circle around the kiva, not meeting anyone's eyes directly, yet making contact with each man. "My people could plant the earth around the mesa to the east where the corn-shaped rock stands watch. This would increase food for both our people."

Winter Moon spoke before anyone else could. "What you say is true. There are many good spots for crops there."

"But it would take most of the day just to walk to the fields and back," Circling Hawk stated, starting his slow movement around the kiva again. "There would be no daylight left for farming." He swept past Walker. "That is why *we* don't farm there. Perhaps your people work best in the darkness."

The snide tone brought Walker's anger to the surface, but he kept his voice even. "When the spring comes, we would ask to settle and build our own village on this second mesa."

"It is Hopi land!" Circling Hawk whirled around, glaring.

Walker met his cold eyes. "No man owns Mother Earth."

"You are both correct in your own way," Winter Moon's words interrupted the rising emotions. "We consider this land as our own, Circling Hawk, but Mother Earth decides who or who will not live upon her. Walker, if your people build a village there, it would be close enough for us to share goods and skills. Both people would benefit."

Winter Moon rose, moving up next to the kiva's stone shrine. He looked down at the small hole dug into the earth in front of the shrine. "Our traditions tell of other clans who climbed out of the holy sipapu from the underworld into this world with our forefathers. Our ancestors were fortunate enough to be allowed to settle here in the center of the universe. The other clans were told they must complete a cycle of migrations to each of the four corners of this land before they could settle upon these mesas. Our *navoti*, prophecies that foretell events of the future, say that each of these clans will return in their own time to build their villages, plant their corn, and raise their children." His eyes fused with Circling Hawk's. "I believe that Walker and his people are one of these returning clans."

Winter Moon paused, drawing deeply on his pipe. He exhaled a cloud of cleansing smoke a second later. "The decision to let them stay must be made by all the clans at Oraibi. We must ponder this and come to an agreement among ourselves, so there will be harmony within our village."

"We appreciate your position. My men and I will wait above in the village." Walker moved to Winter Moon, bent, and blew on his outstretched hand. "Kwa kwa, my brother." He turned and started up the worn log ladder out of the kiva.

It took a few seconds for Walker's eyes to adjust to the bright daylight. He moved away from the kiva entrance to allow the others to come out. Walker blinked his eyes into focus. Oraibi's two- and three-story walls, made of thick slabs of sandstone mortared with mud, wrapped around him on three sides. The village opened up on the steep cliffs of the mesa on the fourth side. To Walker's twentieth-century eye,

Oraibi was the perfect postcard pueblo. To his heart it was home.

Children played in groups around the open plaza. Small Cub, Strong Heart, and Fast Lizard were playing a stone kicking game with some village boys. Women clustered around the first-story doors of the village. Their voices hummed like bees. At a nearby door, Gray Dove, Fawn, and Morning Flower visited with two Hopi women with babies in their arms. The familiar sound of corn being ground in a metate rasped through the cool air. Tall log-pole ladders stretched up to the second- and third-story doors and on up to the rooftops. Men and women sat on the roofs working at various tasks. Nostalgia washed over Walker. The village, faces, and time had changed, but the feeling of home remained the same.

"I think that Winter Moon has more persuasion over the others than Circling Hawk," Scar Cheek said as the men filed up out of the kiva.

Walker nodded. "Winter Moon is a good man with a kind heart, but he is also a wise leader. He will go along with what the others feel is best."

Seeing their men coming out of the kiva, the women started to cluster around. Strong Heart wedged into the tight circle and voiced what the women's eyes asked. "Will they let us stay?"

"They are discussing it now." Walker wished he had sounded more hopeful when he saw the distressed faces around him. "Taawa has walked with us every step of the way here. He could have stopped us with hunger, thirst, or death at any time, but he didn't."

"Walker is correct." Son of Great Bear put his arm

around Morning Flower, squeezing her. "I'm sure this is where we are meant to be and live."

"It might be a long time till word of the decision comes," Walker said to everyone and to no one. "Let's rest and enjoy the village's hospitality till then."

Word came from the kiva with the day's fading light. Walker and his men again found themselves seated in the heart of the village. The kiva fire was larger now to fend off the coldness of the night. Walker tried to swallow the knot of tension in his throat as he listened to Winter Moon speak.

"We, the clan leaders of our village, have come to an agreement." Winter Moon stood by the holy shrine. He spoke to Walker with his eyes and heart. "The decision was not an easy one.

"According to our beliefs, the harmony and well-being of our village must be considered first. We feel that your people seek this same peace and harmony. Our ways also teach us that sharing with others brings happiness to ourselves and to the gods." He turned to Circling Hawk. "But the fear of hunger and thirst haunts our village. Those who have concerns about your people staying have agreed to a peaceful solution."

Winter Moon now talked directly to Walker and his men. "Tomorrow a foot race will be held between our people. Two pahos will be placed on a shrine at the top of the mesa where you desire to settle in the spring. A runner from each people will race to the mesa. If the runner from your people returns first with his prayer stick, then your people will be welcome to share our village and food for the winter. When Mother Earth wakes in the spring, we will help you build a new village near Corn Rock where you . . ."

Circling Hawk broke in. "If *our* runner returns first with his paho, then you and your people will leave our village at the first rays of sun the next day. You will leave the land that we claim as our own and not return." Circling Hawk's narrow eyes gleamed in the firelight.

* * *

A cold wind stung Walker's face as he stood at the edge of the mesa. The smell of moisture filled his nose. Winter was nearer than he wanted to admit. Walker wondered what month it was. December? No, it couldn't be Ka-muyua, the month of the Quiet Moon. During Ka-muyua, there was no digging in the earth, no drum playing, no racing or stamping of feet, not even any loud voices used, because Muyingwa, the Germinating God, was working just beneath the earth's crust. If anything distracted or disturbed Muyingwa, next season's crops would fail and the Hopi would starve.

Walker pulled the turkey feather blanket tighter around his shoulders. It must be late November, he figured, not that it mattered. The concept of hours, months, or years didn't exist among these people. They just lived each minute as it came, lived it as one lived a prayer with faith in higher beings to guide their way. If only he could achieve that peace, that faith. Walker sighed. *If I can just win tomorrow's race.*

Stars sang solos overhead among the dark shadows of the clouds. Peering down over the edge of the steep, rocky mesa, Walker tried to penetrate the darkness. His eyes were useless, but his mind visualized the rugged, high-desert terrain that stretched in all directions. To the southeast stood Second Mesa. He envisioned the small, twentieth-century, village of Mishongnovi, where he had been raised by Náat. In some

155

seven hundred years, Náat would be buried at the foot of Second Mesa in the shadow of Corn Rock. But now, Second Mesa was barren, just waiting for Walker's people to settle there.

*Or was it?*

Would Náat be buried there if Walker didn't win the race tomorrow? How would the future of not only his small band of people but the future of all Hopi people be changed if he lost the race? He pulled the blanket tighter as a shiver of cold crawled up his back and tugged at the nape of his neck. The future of his people again rested squarely on his shoulders.

"Walker."

He had hoped that no one would follow him here. Walker needed time to think, remember, and plan for tomorrow, but at the sound of Flute Maiden's voice he was suddenly glad he wasn't alone. He turned around.

She held out a bowl. "You haven't eaten."

"Kwa kwa." The warmth of the bowl warmed Walker's cold hands.

"Father said the shortest way is always the simplest way." Flute Maiden had assumed his position, staring out into the darkness surrounding the mesa.

Walker nodded. "I wish Great Owl were here to see which is the simplest way." He scooped up some stew with his fingers. It was rich tasting, with small chunks of squash in it. Chewing, Walker gazed again into the dark night. "There are a couple of routes I can take tomorrow. As long as things haven't changed too much, I think I'll have a good chance. Circling Hawk is depending on me not knowing the area, giving his son the advantage."

"The women said Running Cloud is true to his name and

that Circling Hawk wants. . . " Flute Maiden shrugged her shoulders. "There is always someone who is controlled by selfishness." She reached out and touched Walker's arm. "At Lomaki both of *us* were trapped by selfishness—our own and others. Father said you were bound by the people, their needs, and your responsibility. He said that there was little left of you to share with. . ." Her hand fell away from Walker. "Most women are mothers by my age. I felt the web of time wrapping its fingers around me. Silent Thunder became a deadly spider spinning the web tighter and tighter. I wanted to speak, but I couldn't get through my own pride and hurt."

"I thought that you wanted to be with Silent Thunder," Walker whispered, setting the bowl down. "I was too jealous, too angry to see. I should have known."

Flute Maiden shook her head. "When the heart thinks without the mind, or the mind thinks without the heart, then things are not as they should be. There can be no peace with those around us unless there is peace within ourselves first."

Walker gently pulled Flute Maiden to him and held her against his hammering heart. "Taawa created this spot in the universe for those seeking peace. If we, if our people, are to have peace, it will be here at Hopi."

Despite Walker's determination, something deep within him whispered that tomorrow would bring more than just a foot race.

# 20

A low-lying blanket of slate-gray clouds shadowed the late afternoon sun. A winter's wind blew through Walker's leather tunic and leggings. He and his people stood at the edge of the mesa waiting for the race to begin. Walker stamped his feet to keep them warm. "Once I start running, the cold will be welcome," he said, but he saw worry in the eyes of his friends around him.

"The air smells of rain," Scar Cheek said, pulling a rabbit-skin blanket tighter around his shoulders. "If it gets any colder, it will be snow, not rain, that falls, especially if it's night."

Walker tried to sound confident. "I'll be back before dark." He had planned on the race starting much earlier in the day so there would be plenty of daylight. Apparently the leaders of Oraibi didn't share that concern. Walker adjusted the leather strap on the small, dried gourd canteen on his shoulder and tried to keep the worry he felt from showing on his face. Earlier in the day, Winter Moon had given him the gourd, explaining that it was lighter than Walker's ceramic canteen, and had wished him luck in the race.

Small Cub pulled on Walker's sleeve. "Take this." He handed Walker his treasured Boy Scout compass. "Tag said it would never let me get lost. It will help you, too."

Walker looked down and saw his own eyes in the mirror on the back side of the compass. He hardly recognized the lean, tense face peering back at him. Worry lined the weathered skin around his dark, serious eyes. His mouth was tight, his cheeks hollow. He looked closer to twenty-five than fifteen. How could he have changed that much since the day Tag and he walked back into time? Walker's heart twisted. Where was Tag walking now? Was he safe? Had he changed too? The desire to see and laugh with his friend again welled up in Walker. As he turned the compass over, the long, green-and-red needle danced to the north. Walker smiled. A part of Tag would be running with him today. "Kwa kwa, Little Brother. I'll need it and use it." He slipped the compass into his waist pouch.

"People of Oraibi." The village crier's strong voice rang through the cold like a clear bell. "The race between the people of Oraibi and the people of the rocky canyon is about to begin." The message was repeated a second time by the voice that woke the village each morning with a prayer to the cloud people and ended each evening recounting the news of the day.

Men, women, and children climbed down pole ladders and streamed out of first-story doorways. Chattering and laughing, they strolled to where Walker and his people waited at the edge of the mesa.

"Walker," Flute Maiden said as villagers swarmed around them. "Taawa will be with you." Walker read the words on her lips more than heard them against the clamor of the throng.

"Hasn't got a chance . . . "

"Running Cloud has never lost."

"Where will they go?"

The words buzzed like mosquitoes around Walker's ears.

The noisy crowd parted like a curtain and Walker saw Winter Moon approaching. As always, he was smiling. He raised his hand in greetings. Behind Winter Moon, Circling Hawk strutted, accompanied by a young man. The instant Walker saw the sixteen- or seventeen-year-old boy, he knew this was his opponent.

Running Cloud was a good three inches taller in the legs than Walker. He had the lean, disciplined look of the marathon runners of the future—runners who spend hours each day pushing their bodies to the limit and beyond. His loose, yellow tunic and leggings were of finely woven cotton. More aerodynamic than heavy leather, Walker thought, also noting that his competitor wasn't carrying any water or even a knife. *Not a thing to slow him down.*

How many times had Running Cloud won honor and gratuities for his village with his running? America's first professional athlete, Walker thought, seeing the proud smirk on Circling Hawk's face as he approached with his son.

The people closed in around Winter Moon. He climbed on a high rock perched at the edge of the mesa and held up his hand for quiet. "Runners!"

Walker moved next to Running Cloud at the narrow trailhead leading down the mesa. Running Cloud smiled and nodded at Walker. His lean but pleasant square face was relaxed. Anticipation gleamed from his dark, almond-shaped eyes. Walker's thoughts raced. *This is just another Saturday fun run, a chance to do what he loves most—run. He has absolutely nothing to lose.*

Walker forced himself to listen to what Winter Moon was announcing in a loud voice. "Two pahos have now been placed on a shrine at Second Mesa, facing Corn Rock. Both runners have agreed to the rules of this race." Winter Moon looked from Running Cloud to Walker for their nod of public agreement. His eyes rested on Walker. They were apologetic. He lifted a large, white conch shell to his lips. A harsh, loud blare started the race.

For the first few minutes, Walker followed close behind Running Cloud down the steep, narrow path that zigzagged and made sharp turns around boulders and over narrow ledges. Small rocks and dirt flipped back at him like mini-bullets. Dust swirled up into his face. *Eat my dust!* The words popped into Walker's mind. Suddenly Running Cloud pulled ahead and his dust settled before Walker reached it.

*Where is he?* Walker paused at the base of the mesa. His heart was hammering as he panted. Running Cloud was no where in sight.

*It doesn't matter!* Walker told himself and started the route he had plotted out the night before. He would follow the foot of Oraibi's mesa till it ended, then cut straight across the desert floor to the far west side of Second Mesa. He'd climb up the mesa there and run across its flat top to Corn Rock. To Walker, it seemed the simplest route, but apparently Running Cloud hadn't thought so. Had he gone across the long miles of ravine-carved desert floor to the far south side of

Second Mesa and then around to Corn Rock? How much time had Running Cloud spent running the desolate terrain between Oraibi and Second Mesa? Had he worn a smooth path between the two mesas just for such contests? Walker pushed his legs through the pink sand that rested in neat drifts at the foot of the mesa. Sand filled his moccasins.

Walker forced his breathing into a rhythm, with his feet and arms keeping pace. His muscles were beginning to work together now in a flow. The cold wind felt good against his sweating face. The days of hard work and hours of strenuous walking were now paying off. He was in better shape than he had realized. Strategy and luck were all he needed, he told himself. *Strategy and luck!*

He was heading southeast now, a little more south than east. He slipped his hand into his pouch and pulled out Small Cub's compass. *Right on course. Thanks, Tag. Couldn't do it without the compass. Things have changed too much, or should I say, will change in the future.* Walker chuckled. Exhilaration was setting in. He felt great as he ran down the side of a steep wash and up the other side. He leaped over a cactus in his path. Maybe he did have a chance to win.

\* \* \*

*Strategy,* Walker told himself as he pushed hard across the almost-flat terrain. The euphoric feeling that had sustained him the last three or four miles was gone. He was running on more realistic thoughts now. Strategy and *a lot of luck* were the only hopes he had. He had to win. His people's future was at stake. Walker could now see the rocky cliffs of the north finger of Second Mesa. He visualized the wall map of the mesas that had hung in his history class. He had stared at it hundreds of times during all the boring lectures. Three finger-like points made up the southern end of the huge, cropped mountain. The first finger, the one he could see now, curled around and down westward with high, steep cliffs until it blended into the second finger, which also faced west. The rugged sandstone walls of the mesa then wound around eastward to where Corn Rock stood its solitary watch.

*Strategy.* Walker forced his mind to concentrate. Once up the side of the mesa, he would cut eastward across the top of the mesa, then south the five or six miles to where his village would stand someday overlooking Corn Rock.

Walker kept his pace up as he sprinted along the base of the mesa, scanning its steep cliffs and washes for a way up to the top. This was the one area of Second Mesa, due to the distance from his village, that he hadn't explored and hiked as much as others. Now it looked totally alien. The landmarks he had known were nonexistent. He tried to ignore the cold that was penetrating his bones.

*Taawa, you have always guided my way before; please guide it now.* Walker clung to a crack in the rocky face of the mesa. He had followed a faint rabbit path up the side of the mesa, but it had ended nowhere. Countless minutes had been wasted retracing his steps and trying another route up through the rugged cliffs. Now Walker was hanging on for life, searching for another toe hold. A watery curtain formed in his eyes from the cold wind. He fought down the feeling of hopelessness. *Taawa!*

Through the salty veil, he saw a dark spot just above his head. Cautiously, Walker extended his right arm toward it. His fingertips felt the ridge of the crack. He stretched further. His left fingers started to slip. Walker grabbed and made firm contact just as his other hand lost its grip. His foot slipped into a toe hold as if guided by a great hand. Walker's heart felt like it was exploding in his dry mouth. He forced himself to search the sandstone for another finger hold.

A drizzle of icy rain washed Walker's face as he ran eastward along the top of the mesa. His legs were cramping from the strain of rock climbing and the cold. Pushing harder, Walker tried not to think about the precious minutes he had lost climbing up. He was in his own territory now—or at least it had been his in the future. His uncle had pushed him out the door each day, saying, "Go. You must learn our mountaintop as you know your own hands." There wasn't a nook or cranny Walker hadn't explored or a rabbit trail or path he hadn't followed to its end. If there was a chance for him to pull ahead of Running Cloud it was here.

The low sun was shrouded by thick clouds. Premature darkness was filling the air. Walker reached up and pushed a wet strand of hair out of his eyes as he forced his aching legs forward. A large rock formation emerged ahead through the rain. Walker recognized it as the one he had played on as a child. Corn Rock was less than a half mile away!

Deadly silence met Walker as he ran into the area where the plaza of his future village, Mishongnovi, would stand. The icy rain ceased to fall as if deflected by unseen powers. A frigid wind whirled around him. In its breath, Walker heard a faint sound. He skidded to a stop. A chill shot up his spine.

Drums beat softly.

Walker whirled around and saw nothing but cloud-laden sky and barren land. The sound drew closer, growing louder. Walker's fear eased as he heard the cadence coupled with the distinctive rattling of dried gourds filled with pebbles. Walker closed his eyes and listened as the wind carried the music closer. Antelope hooves clacked rhythmically against tortoise shells. Walker's left foot began keeping time. The air vibrated with deep, throaty voices of Kachinas singing a prayer song. He felt the air rush around him as each guardian spirit danced by and around him in a long line. The sounds, the words, the passion vibrated through Walker, warming, comforting, and strengthening. His spirit soared.

One by one the drums, rattles, and songs receded into the wind. Walker opened his eyes to emptiness. The freezing wind gnawed at his body, but the warmth in his heart remained.

Walker lifted his face to the clouds. "Great Taawa, I will win this race! This ground will be a place where the Kachinas will dance for hundreds of years to come."

It took only minutes for him to spot the small stone shrine nestled beside three distinctive red rocks that looked at Corn Rock below. Reaching the shrine, Walker's heart stopped.

A single paho lay on the shrine. Running Cloud had already been there and gone. Icy rain stung Walker's face. Realization bit at his pounding heart, while the crystal of hope he had clung to shattered. Hot anger sprang up in its place. Circling Hawk's gloating face burst into Walker's mind, stoking the anger.

*Strategy.* There was no luck now. His original plan was to backtrack, since it had seemed the shortest way. Now he knew it would be easier to go down this side of the mesa. He had done it thousands of times, getting water and going to school.

With the paho tucked in his belt, Walker started down. The memorized, well-worn trails of the future didn't exist.

*Fine, I will just start one right now, since my people are going to live here one way or another! Circling Hawk has no rightful claim on this land.* Walker could barely see the ground beneath his feet in the darkness, but he pushed forward harder, faster.

*We'll just take the land. It may be the first time someone takes Hopi land, but it certainly won't be the last!*

Walker stumbled off into the sand dunes at the foot of the mesa. *I'll follow the mesa around to the west until it starts going north again, then cross over the desert floor to Oraibi.* He wished that there were stars to help guide his way, but they were covered in thick clouds. As long as he had the mesa to follow he would be alright, but the miles of open land between the two mesas would be treacherous. What landmarks Walker knew would be unrecognizable in the darkness. He'd be traveling on instinct. Even the compass would be useless without light. If only he had a torch—or his flash light!

The bottom of his feet seared with each pounding step. His legs ached with fatigue, his lungs burned white. As Walker rounded the last finger of the mesa, the icy wind whipped the sound of angry voices into Walker's face. He dropped down close to the wet ground beside a huge rock and listened.

"He understands what we're saying. He just doesn't want to tell us anything. We're wasting time. Let's just kill him and start back home." The familiar voice came from behind huge boulders huddled at the foot of the mesa a few feet away.

"I'm hungry," Slow Bear's thick voice answered. "Let me

kill him now so we can eat in peace before it starts to rain again."

Grateful for the darkness that covered his movement, Walker edged himself up a boulder and peered over. Ten feet away, Slow Bear, Black Spider, and Tangled Grass crouched around a large fire built against another clump of rocks. Just a few feet away, Running Cloud sat with his back to Walker. His hands were bound behind him.

*Strategy and luck.*

Here were opportunities for both. Winning the race was now within Walker's reach.

# 21

Walker eased himself down and lay against the side of the rough boulder. His heart hammered, and his mind raced as he listened.

"What do we tell Silent Thunder?" Tangled Grass demanded.

Black Spider's voice carried in the bitter wind. "The truth. That we didn't find the medicine woman or her people. The witches killed them just like they did Walker."

"Tell me again," Slow Bear's sluggish voice said, "about the bones that glowed."

"Be quiet!" Black Spider snapped.

Walker peered over the top of his hiding place. Fear and tension swirled in the wind as the men huddled around the fire.

Slow Bear pushed, "Was the boy who flies in time really dead? And was the witch sucking blood from his heart?"

"Oh-ay! He is two-hearted, a witch now," said Tangled Grass.

"Both of you be quiet!" Black Spider threw a piece of wood into the fire. In the dancing firelight, he looked nervous.

"I'm hungry. Let me kill the Hopi so we can eat without guarding him," Slow Bear said.

"He's right, Black Spider. The boy is no use to us. Let's get it done and start back." Tangled Grass said. "If Silent Thunder wants the medicine woman, let him hunt for her. I'm tired of sleeping on the cold ground."

*Strategy and luck.* The words echoed through Walker's mind. Anger still warmed his body. All he had to do was slip away and make it back to Oraibi. It would be easy, and the future of his people would be won fair and square. It was Running Cloud's father who had set up the race. Circling Hawk knew full well that Walker didn't have a chance. Well, now he had a chance. All he had to do was seize it and run!

Walker slid down the boulder.

"Let me kill him," pleaded Slow Bear. "I'll just twist his neck like a turkey's . . . "

A shudder shook Walker. His stomach twisted with nausea. White Badger's strong but ashen face flashed in his mind. Walker's throat tightened. Rage began boiling within him, heated by the memory of White Badger's crushed neck.

*Strategy.* The word fought through to Walker's logic.

Think!

*Strategy . . .*

Nothing came.

Think harder. Walker's hand went to his knife. One knife against three. *Useless.* What else did he have?

*Taawa, please . . .* Walker stopped.

What did one pray for when seeking to destroy others, even if they were going to kill another innocent person? *Justice. Capital punishment.* He forced the bahana's words away, although he was sure Taawa understood them. His body trembled.

What did he have without Taawa's help?

Walker reached into his waist pack. Tag's compass rubbed against his finger. *Possibly.*

He felt the oval lightning stones beneath the compass. *Maybe.* Taking out the three objects, Walker tried to concentrate. The lightning stones—would they work? Doubt nagged Walker. Some magnetic force or something had to be present to produce the rocks' illumination. *Darkness broken by the whiteness of bones.* Shell Listener's words erased away all of Walker's twentieth-century logic. There were no bones here— yet. Walker slipped the rocks back into his pouch.

That left Tag's compass. How would Tag use the futuristic instrument and its mirror against three primitive men? Tag's grinning, freckled face burst into Walker's mind. *Let them see what they really are!*

Walker's breath caught in his throat. The freezing air beat against his bare chest as he pulled off his tunic. He could hear the three still debating over killing Running Cloud. Walker stripped off his leggings. His loincloth did nothing to keep the cold out. He retied his belt around his waist and stuck his knife in it. The knife felt warm against his cold skin.

Walker slithered along the cold, wet ground on his stomach. It took only seconds for him to reach Running Cloud. Still lying on the ground, keeping his eyes on the three huddled at the fire, Walker cut the cords that bound Running Cloud's wrists. Running Cloud didn't move as he felt the pull of the knife.

"We've wasted enough time!" Black Spider cried. "Just kill him."

Slow Bear lumbered to his feet and started toward Running Cloud. Walker sprang up with a primeval scream that chilled his own blood. With a loud, crackling laugh, he leap-frogged over Running Cloud, landing in an animalistic crouch. Slow Bear froze, one foot in front of the other. Black Spider and Tangled Grass vaulted to their feet.

Walker jerked himself up to full height. He stomped toward the three. Terror paralyzed the men.

"You first, big one. Becoming two-hearted takes only a blink of the eye," Walker screeched as he lunged at Slow Bear, landing inches away from him. He flashed open his hand and pushed the compass mirror into the huge man's face. Slow Bear stumbled backward. His eyes were unable to tear themselves from the ugly, firelit reflection glaring back at him in the palm of Walker's hand. Little gurgles came from his throat as he stared at himself in the mirror.

Beyond, the other two were like rocks. "Look deep, Slow Bear. Your soul is mine." Walker thrust his other hand at Slow Bear's chest. "Now for your heart!"

"No!" The word sounded like a terrified child's. Slow Bear whirled around, tripped, scrambled back up, bounded past the others, and disappeared into the night.

Walker flew at Tangled Grass with the mirror extended out. "Your spirit is next!" Tangled Grass's face was white. His body shook so badly that Walker was amazed he could run so fast.

Black Spider was out of sight before Walker took a step in his direction. "I have your souls," Walker shrieked, "and I will hunt you wherever you go until I have your hearts! There is no place that I can't follow!" The wind whipped his vow after the three men.

Heavy raindrops beat down on Walker's bare shoulders. The fire popped and sizzled. He had to get his clothes back on. Witches may not need them, but he certainly did. There was no sign of Running Cloud. Walker pulled on his leggings and grabbed the paho from where it lay. How much of his act had Running Cloud seen? Realization washed over him with the frigid rain. If Running Cloud believed he was a two-hearted witch, it wouldn't matter who won the race. Had he saved Running Cloud's life at the cost of his people's future? Cold shook his body in spasmodic waves.

Taking precious minutes, Walker scattered the men's packs into the darkness, just in case they came back looking for them. In the firelight, he checked the compass for the direction to Oraibi. He was tempted to make a torch, but if the three regained their courage, which he doubted, a torch would be a beacon. Walker threw dirt on the fire. Wet, cold darkness saturated the wintry night once more.

The first few minutes of running, Walker's muscles refused to cooperate. He recognized, or thought he did, a ravine. Good, he was still on course. But could he stay on course in the stark darkness? It would be all to easy to get lost. If only I could see—see with inner sight, Walker thought. *If only* . . .

How long had he been running? Walker wiped the water from his brow before it dripped into his eyes. It felt like hours but was probably minutes. His legs and thighs screamed with pain. His moccasins were wet all the way through, and his toes were going numb. The temperature was dropping by the minute. The rain was an icy sheet that he could barely see through. He wasn't even sure whether he was going in the right direction now. Walker tried to force his mind—his inner sight—to see through the all-consuming darkness of the night. Muddy, obscure shadows filled his mind. Frustration exploded within Walker, obliterating the veiled images in his mind.

Walker heard moaning a second before he saw the slithering mass on the muddy ground. Fear catapulted more adrenaline into his body. In the next instant he recognized his racing opponent and crouched beside him. "Running Cloud."

"I was going for help, but . . ." Running Cloud's voice broke with pain.

"What did they do?"

"Broke my fingers and toes."

Walker helped Running Cloud to a sitting position. "Why didn't you just tell them about me so they wouldn't hurt you?"

"They wanted a boy who flew through time. You can barely run."

Walked laughed and shook his head. "I'm not that bad." He slipped his arm under Running Cloud. "We've got to keep going or freeze." Walker was afraid of shock and hypothermia. Running Cloud's thin cotton clothes were drenched. He was shaking like a leaf. Walker was amazed that between the pain and the cold he had gotten this far. Running Cloud cried out as he put weight on his feet. Walker wished with all his heart that he could fly—fly both of them to warm, dry safety.

Each yard seemed like a mile to Walker. He knew that it was worse for Running Cloud as he hobbled along. Going up and down the countless gullies was the hardest. Running Cloud's arms would tighten on his neck and shoulder, and Walker felt almost all of Running Cloud's weight upon him then.

*Taawa, give us strength . . .*

The rain turned into a thick, icy slush. Walker's feet were numb. How many toes would they lose to frostbite? Would either of them ever run again? He pushed the grim possibility away. Positive thoughts, good thoughts, he told himself, but he couldn't dredge any up.

Walker tried to keep Running Cloud talking, to keep tabs on his mental condition. Confusion was a sign of hypothermia. "You must have run at night before."

"The stars are good running companions," Running Cloud said. "Not the rain."

"At least we will be clean."

Running Cloud's body shook. "Rather be warm."

"We'll be both soon." Walker said. *That is, if we are going in the right direction,* his mind cautioned. He kept Running Cloud talking of running, hunting, planting, of warmth, food, and family.

Walker's fingers were now numb. How long had they been walking? Minutes and hours all bled together as they fought to keep going through the blinding rain and darkness.

Running Cloud pulled to a stop. "Where are we?"

"On our way home," Walker tried to sound confident. Was hypothermia finally taking over Running Cloud?

"I have been here before," Running Cloud cried.

Walker tried to move on. "Oh-ay, you've run here before."

"No! We're going in circles," Running Cloud insisted, pulling back on Walker. "We're going in circles!"

Walker strained to see the surroundings. Running Cloud was right! They had crossed this same gully before. How could they have gotten turned around? Were they both suffering from the disorienting effects of hypothermia? Walker fought the panic rising within him. Where were they? Where was Oraibi? How much time did they have before Masau'u closed his fingers around them in freezing death?

"Great Taawa, help us!" Walker cried but didn't hear his voice against the darkness of the night.

*You must use your inner sight.* Great Owl's words whispered through the turmoil and fear in his mind.

"How?" Walker screamed, again not hearing his desperate cry.

*Rid your heart of anger and hatred. Humble yourself that you may be in harmony and peace.* The answer had the power of lightning.

Before Walker could react, Running Cloud crumpled to the ground, pulling Walker down with him. "Circles, going in circles, lost—lost," he moaned.

Kneeling beside Running Cloud, Walker lifted his face to the sky. Icy rain beat against his closed eyes. "Great Taawa, please help cleanse my heart of the anger and hatred that has driven me for the last months. Let me find the peace that I have sought for so many years." Tears warmed Walker's freezing cheeks. His heart felt like it was breaking into pieces. "Please Taawa, help me use the inner sight that you have given me. Let me see for the good of my people!"

A dim image began to form in Walker's mind. Tag's silver compass became clearer as Walker prayed for inner balance and peace. The compass needle pointed through the darkness.

Walker struggled to his feet, pulling Running Cloud up with him. Rain now fell in a blinding, freezing torrent, but Walker could see the compass needle clearly in his mind. He focused all his energy on the needle as he half-carried, half-dragged Running Cloud along.

"Kwa kwa, Taawa, kwa kwa," Walker prayed. The image of the compass was sharp in his mind as they treaded through the mud, cacti, and rocks for what seemed like an eternity.

The rain stopped with an eerie abruptness. A wind that cut deep into the soul and bones took its place. Walker felt the mud thicken into ice beneath his numb feet. Running Cloud's weight became heavier with each step. *One foot at a time . . . just one foot in front of the other*, he told himself, as he struggled to keep the compass needle in his sight.

The compass needle began to fade minutes later as the wind whipped harder against Walker and Running Cloud. Desperation began to fill Walker's mind until he saw the massive rocks that lay strewn around the foot of the mesa. His sight had led him through the darkness! "Running Cloud, we've made it! All we need to do is climb up to the village," Walker shouted. No longer focusing on his inner sight, Walker became acutely aware of his numb body. He had never been so cold before in his life.

Running Cloud moaned in pain with the first step up the sharp incline. Walker slid on the icy path. They both fell in a heap on the rocky ground. The wind's howl covered Running Cloud's cry as his broken fingers slammed into the ground.

Pain seared Walker's brittle, cold skin and bones. His mind drifted above the pain. A strange warmth penetrated his body. He just wanted to curl up into a tight ball against the freezing wind and sleep. *Sleep.* Walker fought the overwhelming impulse and struggled to his feet. "We've got to keep going."

The steep path was a wind-blown sheet of ice. Walker battled to keep his own footing while supporting Running Cloud. With his free hand, he clung to rocks along the side of the path. The wind beat against them with each slow step.

Running Cloud slipped. Walker grabbed him with both hands. The icy ground came up fast. Pain shot through Walker's body.

It would be faster if he left Running Cloud here, climbed up to the village and got help, Walker realized trying to sit up. It was impossible for just one person to get Running Cloud up the icy path.

Yes, that is what he had do. Walker forced his aching bones up. He looked down at Running Cloud, crumbled up in a ball. The smell of death swirled in the wind that roared through Walker's body. Masau'u was at his shoulder.

"No! I won't let you take Running Cloud," Walker cried as he pulled Running Cloud to his feet and began inching upward again.

Nothing seemed real now. It was all a nightmare that Walker wanted desperately to wake up from. His feet slipped, but he caught himself and fought to keep Running Cloud upright.

Suddenly, Running Cloud's weight was lifted.

*Masau'u!* Fear blinded Walker. "No!" he screamed, fighting to keep hold of Running Cloud.

"Walker," Masau'u was using Scar Cheek's voice to trick him.

Walker hurdled himself over Running Cloud. "No, Masau'u!" He forced his eyes tight against the face of death. Masau'u started to pry his body off Running Cloud, but Walker held on with his own death grip. "I will not let you take him!"

"Walker, it's Son of Great Bear."

Scar Cheek's voice followed. "Walker, you'll both die if you don't let us help."

Walker looked down at the hands pulling on his arms. They were flesh and blood, with deep scars running across them.

Scar Cheek and Son of Great Bear struggled up the last few yards of the icy path with Running Cloud between them. Walker watched them crest the path. He stopped and lifted his face to the sky. "Kwa kwa, Great Taawa."

Cheers came from the top of the trail. Walker pushed himself over the rim of the mesa. A fire burned bright against the night. A small crowd of men gathered around Running Cloud, who was still being held up by Scar Cheek and Son of Great Bear. Flute Maiden, with her medicine bag, was trying to get to Running Cloud. Walker's other men and Strong Heart stood in a tight circle, watching.

"Running Cloud is the winner!" Circling Hawk's sharp voice screeched over the wind. He stood close to his son. His voice rose even louder as he swung around and pointed at Walker at the edge of the crowd now. "You and your people will leave with the first light of . . . "

"No!" Running Cloud's voice rose over his father's declaration.

Circling Hawk whirled around to face his son.

"No, Father." Running Cloud pulled away from those holding him up and stood on his own. "I did not win. The winner must have a paho from the shrine." He held up his mangled hands. "I have no paho."

Walker felt all eyes on him. The only sound he heard was the fire's crackling and his own heart's thunder. Walker reached down to his belt. The eagle feathers on the paho blew against his fingertips.

# 22

With the first rays of the sun on his face, Walker felt the promise of spring. Keeping his eyes closed, he let the sun's warmth drift through his chilled body as its energy bolstered his spirit. His heart overflowed with the gratitude that he had just expressed in his morning prayer. This would be a good day.

Still kneeling, Walker opened his eyes to the beauty of the sun rising over Second Mesa. He spat over his shoulder, cleansing himself. "Kwa kwa, Great Taawa," Walker said one more time and rose.

He gazed down to the foot of the mesa, where their village was plotted out. Large sandstone rocks marked the corners of each of the one-room, adjoining houses. Walker and his men had gone to a Hopi priest, each obtaining four eagle feathers. These feathers were laid beneath the corner stones of their homes as prayer offerings. A fine trail of white cornmeal and herbs showed where the walls of each house were to be built. Members of Winter Moon's and Running Cloud's clans were coming today to help Walker's people begin to build the thick sandstone-and-mud walls.

It was a small village, but it would grow one family at a time. Walker smiled. During the last moon, Running Cloud had spent much of his time at the grinding room window, courting Scar Cheek's oldest daughter, Fluttering Bird. Running Cloud's uncle was already spending many days in the kiva weaving an oov, a white wedding robe, for Fluttering Bird. As soon as the oov was completed, and the needed cornmeal ground and other gifts prepared, there would be another wedding. It will be good to have Running Cloud as a neighbor, Walker thought.

Studying the charted-out village below, Walker again wished that it was going to be built here on top of the mesa. He took a deep breath and let it out slowly, remembering how hard it had been to make the decision to build below. It was so beautiful, so safe, here on the mesa top. But he had let his people decide together where to build, forcing his knowledge of the future aside. Their water source was at the foot of the mesa, and so were the areas they would farm. Walker sighed. Yes, life would be easier below, for now.

A chill crept up Walker's spine. *For now* . . . His sight took over his mind in a whirl of images and knowledge. In some three hundred years, the Spanish would come with their horrible oppressions—killings, whippings, cutting off of fingers and toes, starvings, and forbidding of Kachina dances, all in the name of Christianity. These barbaric cruelties and others would force his posterity to relocate to the top of the mesa for protection.

*Three hundred years!*

It seemed like an eternity, but it would come, all too soon. A heaviness tore at Walker's heart as his eyes saw further into the future. The vision of Spanish priests being thrown off the cliffs of Oraibi to their deaths in 1680 played through Walker's mind in shadows of black and red. Walker saw the bahanas come, bringing a different kind of oppression—unalterable laws, alien religions, paved roads, schools, welfare, electricity, television, and all their compulsive, time-oriented ways.

Time . . . Walker thought. Time is nothing more than a blink of an eye, a concept that can be walked.

*Hopivewat, the Hopi way, is not concerned with hours, days, or years. Hopivewat is only concerned with living in peace within ourselves and those around us. Think happy thoughts, good thoughts; time will take care of itself.* Náat's often-spoken words broke through the swirling images and thoughts in Walker's mind.

"You are right," Walker whispered, forcing his mind and eyes back to the fluffy clouds hovering over the sacred mountain on the far horizon to the southwest.

"Right about what?"

Flute Maiden's voice startled Walker. He swung around and found her a foot away. A new warmth surged through him. "Right to have you as my wife." He moved to her and put his arms around her. Her hair still smelled of the yucca ,soap used to wash their hair at their wedding yesterday.

Holding Flute Maiden against him, Walker was overwhelmed with love and the need to protect her. A wave of fear and anxiety swelled in his chest. What if Silent Thunder did come looking for Flute Maiden? What if she got sick or hurt? Could he grow enough food to keep her stomach full—

and the stomachs of their children to come? The thought of the peril of childbirth increased Walker's fears. His knees felt weak. He clung to Flute Maiden more tightly. How could he protect her from all the everyday dangers in this primitive life? *How?* his frightened mind screamed. *How?*

Tag's freckled face suddenly burst into Walker's mind, crushing his worries about Flute Maiden. Tag's face was twisted in fear. His mouth called inaudible words.

*You must walk time again.* Great Owl's words blocked out Tag's image, leaving Walker's body shaking.

"When?" The desperate words escaped Walker's lips.

"Walker?" Flute Maiden touched his cheek. "What are you seeing?"

"Not seeing, hearing." Walker pulled her close. Her heart beat against his own, adding her courage to his. He knew without a doubt that he must walk time again to help his bahana friend who was playing a deadly game of tag against time. When he was to leave was not clear yet. When the time came, he would have to depend on his inner sight to guide him and on Great Owl's paho to open the doors of time.

He gazed over Flute Maiden's head at the beautiful, vast land below. He felt its beauty, its tranquillity.

Hopi.

Peace again settled in his heart, despite the ghost of fear that lingered in his brain.

*Walker of Time.* Náat's dying words danced in the morning's gentle breeze. *Do what must be done . . . Come home to Hopi.*

Walker answered, "It is done . . . for now."

# *More High-Adventure Titles for Young Adult Readers*

## THE KEYMAKER: Born to Steal
### by Penny Porter

Jimmy Cooper, a teenager trapped in a home life that is out of control, chooses to use his talent as a locksmith for easy money and crime. As the story unfolds, Jimmy has to face the emotional and practical conflicts which are the consequences of this choice.

160 pages, 5 1/4 x 7 1/2, Ages 12 and up   Pbk ISBN 0-943173-99-X   $10.95

## WALKER OF TIME
### by Helen Hughes Vick

A compelling, fact-based mystery about a teenage Hopi Indian boy who "time travels" back to A.D.1250, and the final days of his ancestors in the cliff-dwellings of northern Arizona.

"The dialogue is clever, the pacing suspenseful, and the style smooth. . . ."
*Booklist*, Sept. 1993

192 pages, 5 1/4 x 7 1/2, Ages 12 and up   Pbk ISBN 0-943173-80-9   $9.95

## SON-OF-THUNDER
### by Stig Holmas

A young Apache warrior, adopted into the family of Cochise and Geronimo, achieves manhood during a time of great conflict and change.  Told from the Apache point of view to balance more conventional historical accounts.

"Interesting. deeply sympathetic, vivid portrayal." --*Kirkus Review*, Nov. 1993

128 pp, 5 1/4 x 7 1/2, Ages 12 and up
Pbk ISBN 0-943173-87-6   $10.95   HC ISBN 0-943173-88-4   $16.95

### *To order, simply contact*
### *your favorite bookseller or distributor.*

# Harbinger House
### *Books of Integrity*
TUCSON